NEELKAMAL PURI was born in Ludhiana, Punjab. She now lives in Chandigarh, where she teaches English literature and media studies at the Post Graduate Government College for Girls. She is the author of two novels: The Patiala Quartet and Remember to Forget.

Remember
to
forget

NEEL KAMAL PURI

SPEAKING
TIGER

SPEAKING TIGER PUBLISHING PVT. LTD
4381/4, Ansari Road, Daryaganj
New Delhi - 110002

First published in 2012 by Rupa Publications India
This edition first published by Speaking Tiger 2015
Copyright © Neel Kamal Puri 2012, 2015

ISBN: 978-93-85755-37-8

eISBN: 978-93-85755-33-0

10 9 8 7 6 5 4 3 2 1

To my sister Dodi,

for the many heart-to-hearts.

1

The iced whisky in the glass had numbed Tejpal's hand into a talon. He transferred the glass to his left hand and blew hard on the right one. The fingers gradually woke to life when his foggy breath touched them.

As the evening shivered on, the air above the nearby Sirhind Canal condensed into water droplets. They gathered in a puddle on top of the tent that had been pitched for the party. When the tent could take no more, it slowly started letting down its burden. A number of drops squeezed through the canvas and suspended themselves there, waiting to gather strength. Then one droplet took a tentative plunge into the plush seating underneath, and others, sure of finding a soft landing, quickly followed suit. The pearly procession began to make a joyous descent.

There was a noisy rout underneath. The women went 'Eeeee' and jumped up; the men went straight to the point with a series of 'sisterfuckers' and 'motherfuckers' muttered under their breaths. Guests scattered looking for cover, or at least a place near the numerous coal fires placed for the women to warm their hands and the men their frozen posteriors.

It was not a great time to party, since November is a

cold month. The sunshine is only a decoy. At night, the cold is real, becoming gooseflesh on naked arms in party clothes on garden chairs. Most people had forgotten the cold of last November and the November before that and the one even before that. 'It was not so cold last November,' they told each other, even though it had been just as cold if not colder. However, it was important to forget, to move on.

And one way of doing that was to run a party relay, a series of parties, each edging the previous one out of the frame with the spectacle that it offered. Insurgency in the state was in its dying throes and what better time than this, to celebrate? They had just lived through ten years of police clampdowns and curfews. Men with long beards and equally long names—names that carried their addresses, following the nineteenth-century edict on using the name of the village of birth as the surname—and an even longer list of dos and don'ts, had curbed the natural excesses of the Punjabi spirit. Their dos had included carving Khālistān out of the Indian state. And their don'ts had forbidden liquor, among a lot of other things. In fact, there were a hundred and twenty-two 'thou shalt nots', proclaimed from mikes at religious congregations, posters on gurdwara walls, press notes that landed on the newspaper editor's table with a warning—print or else…

They proscribed make-up and nose rings and earrings and bangles for brides. They proscribed salwars for boys because boys must be boys and wear the pants in the family.

They prescribed veils for the women to cover their heads with.

They proscribed shedding tears for the dead. Or bowing before the dead.

They prescribed telling on those who were telling on them to the police. They also prescribed food and shelter for themselves if they were to visit villages in the dead of the night.

They proscribed girls dancing on stage.

They proscribed Hindi and the national anthem.

They prescribed death for policemen, informers, dogs that barked in the night, stubborn newspaper editors, men who did not wear turbans... It was a long list.

In these ten years people had been dying of fear rather than in the appropriate Punjabi way—of high cholesterol induced by a desi ghee diet... Until the long-bearded ones themselves began to party and decay. Some of them were discovered living under false identities, in houses equipped with twenty-four televisions and video players, twelve mixies, ten air conditioners, thirty-two cameras and on and on, a long list of gratuitous greed.

However, the state police kept suggesting that it might be wiser to wait a while before celebrating. They said so to the industrialists of Ludhiana specifically, one of them being Mr Bakshi, owner of a hosiery factory. But Mr Bakshi's event managers had suggested 'Snow' as a party theme. This idea would have been a bit incongruous in summer. Of necessity it had to be done in winter, and then, better November than December when it would become even colder.

The venue was Mr Bakshi's home, which had been modelled on a house that he had seen in Europe. Reigning local architectural taste had been added to it—Gothic columns and Roman domes, modernist angularity and Georgian windows, Islamic minarets and English roofs. One dish of everything on your menu, please.

This evening, very little of the house was visible, with

the rising fog clouding it out of existence. The fog had risen from the fields drenched in irrigation. It usually hung above the experimental fields of the Punjab Agricultural University before slyly spreading its reach in whispered movements. Mr Bakshi's house had been swallowed whole.

Lights, with their outlines untidily rubbed out by the fog, lit the way. Pebbled pieces of thermocol formed a snowy carpet all along the driveway from the gate to the doorstep. Rectangular strips of cotton wool hung like limp bandages from the branches of trees and plants, which were otherwise bare of foliage. Attempts had been made at providing the sloping English roof with a thermocol and cotton cover, but most of it had just roller-coasted its way down to the ground.

'Enjoying?' Mr Bakshi asked Tejpal when he spotted him standing alone, flexing his fingers.

It was a usage Mr Bakshi had picked up from a prostitute he had visited in his youth. He had been reluctant to give her his name for fear of having it sullied and had introduced himself as Pappu, a name that gave away absolutely nothing, a name that had neither prefix nor suffix. He was just one pappu amongst thousands of other anonymous pappus out there—who were anything from waiters in dhabas to insurance agents to big industrialists to politicians.

'Enjoying, Pappu?' she had asked at the height of his ecstasy.

And since then it had seemed such a well-worded question, so fulsome. Now he omitted the Pappu, though.

'Enjoying?' he asked Tejpal again. 'Have a drink-shrink,' he added. At other times, or earlier in the evening, it would have been 'tea-shee'. The doggerel came from effusive heartiness, from a hospitality that pinned you down and forced food down your throat. Just the offer of a drink was an inadequate, pale statement of intent.

Tejpal was not 'enjoying', because November was that one month of the year which he did not like. He did not like most months, but this one in particular was where his nightmares were temporally located. It was always November when he was startled awake from his sleep and had to wipe a film of perspiration from his forehead.

'Yes, enjoying,' he said, though his tongue involuntarily, yet again, sought and probed the cavity in his molar, and his senses waited for the familiar pain that would jangle through his head. I really must go to a dentist, he thought; but that required concerted action and he had, in any case, got used to the pain. It was only occasionally that the pain became loud enough for him to think of the dentist. It was a bad moment to be asked if he was 'enjoying'.

Perhaps it was also Mr Bakshi's attitude and his distracted, disinterested air that prickled under Tejpal's skin. But then these moments don't have a single trigger. They come from an accumulated backlog of resentments and memories, from the last word you never got in during an argument, from the up-yours sign that the speeding motorist left with you before he became dust in the distance. One of those moments may choose, maybe, 10.20 p.m. on the first of November to erupt.

'Good, good,' said Mr Bakshi, rubbing his hands together in the certainty of a thing going well, already on his way to the stage to catch some of the limelight.

'You could not find any other day to have this party?' Tejpal said, grabbing Mr Bakshi's retreating shoulder just a shade roughly.

'Is there something wrong with today?'

'You have forgotten the riots of November 1984, when so many Sikhs were slaughtered?'

'That was ten years ago, Tej beta.'

'They split open our skulls, they gouged out our eyes, they poured kerosene on us and burnt us alive. Thousands of Sikhs died that day. Just because it was ten years ago does not mean you...' Language was beginning to desert Tejpal. The sentence completed itself in a number of popping sounds that must have approximated a sentiment.

'You have to learn to go on with your life,' Mr Bakshi advised him. This was his favourite counsel, the one that allowed him to go back to the miracle of his own rejuvenation. Once upon a time, his mother had always apologized for having to entertain without carpets. 'All ours have gone for dry cleaning, you see.' The sorrow of not having any carpets killed her. How happy she would have been today to see all the carpets in his house. Even in the bathrooms! Carpets with foam lining underneath, like padded bras. She might have been happier still with the swathes of marble that formed white vistas in his house, with the pearl and satin-finished woodwork and the golden cornices.

He was about to say more. 'To be very frank...' was going to be his next line, as it so often was. But Tejpal's brow was much too thunderous and his eyes too raw red for any 'frankly' friendly chats. He was not in the mood to hear any preaching. He was in the mood to sock someone in the jaw. He made a wild figure just now. His open beard was flowing down to his chest, his saffron turban looked like it would ignite from the spark of his anger. This had been his new look after November 1984, when he had begun to see himself as the keeper of his religion, and the groomed corporate image had given way to the Punjabi Wild West.

✷

There was a time when he had sported a close-cropped beard and short hair, quite against the tenets of his religion. But that was long before everyone became jumpy about matters of religion; before they lost their sense of humour. Before the capers of the comedian in Sikh garb in a Hindi film evoked not laughter, but indignation. Travelling by train, he had happened to be sharing his compartment with a lumdarrhiya, a longbeard, an irreverent reference to a very devout Sikh. The lumdarrhiya had quizzed him about his religion.

'Beta, you must not trim your beard or cut your hair. The guru had created the Khalsa, the Sikh, in his own image. "Khalsa mero rup hae," he had said.' The lumdarrhiya had quoted him scriptures. 'You have committed a grave sin. A very grave sin.' He shook his admonishing finger at Tejpal, then topped it up with some wisdom. 'You know that each hair of the head, each pore that houses that hair, receives signals from the guru. When you cut off that hair, you cut off your direct connection with the guru,' he said, stroking his own beard with a flourish that was designed to provoke envy of his high connectivity with the heavens. He then leaned over and whispered to him that women who shave their underarms similarly destroy these celestial transmitters.

Tejpal had punctured the pompousness with a strategically told untruth.

'Singhji, I was born a Hindu and was in the process of converting to Sikhism out of a belief in its tolerance and modernity, but listening to you today has convinced me that

I might as well go back to the faith of my ancestors.'

That had deflated Singhji, who had then practically prostrated himself at Tejpal's feet, asking to be forgiven for his unbidden tirade and begging him not to revoke his decision to convert to Sikhism.

The Singhji would be happy to see him today, with his flowing beard, each hair receiving godly messages, though reason had become bits of flying debris from the fiery explosion inside his head.

Tejpal made a lunge for Mr Bakshi, saying, 'Doesn't matter to you, does it? You are a mona, a Hindu.'

These days everyone was trying to negotiate the narrow spaces between religious identities, talking about the weather instead of counting the number of Hindus killed by the long-bearded Sikhs through the years of insurgency, or the number of Sikhs killed by Hindu hooligans in the riots of November 1984. There were official statistics for each of these categories. Statistics to prove that the terrorists had killed as many Sikhs as Hindus; others to prove that the riots were as much an expression of the distance between those who were flush with effete and those who would like nothing better than to be that way. Interpretations could absolve one side and indict the other or vice versa. Statistics were putty but life was not.

To give the acrimony a voice and form was luring the snake out of its hole. And maybe sticking one's own finger in it too, for good measure.

Tejpal had clearly crossed a boundary.

An irked Mr Bakshi said, 'What is this Hindu-Hindu? You are not the only one to have been in the middle of riots. I have seen enough riots in my time.' He said it as though it were a well-cultivated virtue.

Mr Bakshi knew, though he did not know how to say it, that you could not feed off God. No matter what the promises of the afterlife, God was not going to get up and cook dal makhni and top it up with a desi ghee tadka when your stomach growled. These Sikhs, he thought, they really could be a bit dense sometimes. It was from the perpetual weight of the turban maybe. But he did not want to be caught with that thought and quickly shook it out of his head.

By now Tejpal's voice had risen many uncomfortable decibels while various pairs of hands tried to restrain him. He bellowed a series of sputtering incomprehensibles about discrimination against the Sikhs, about Punjab's river waters flowing into other states, about Sikh jokes.

The male half of the gathering congealed around this sudden sore, rushing in emergency measures.

✖

Tejpal's wife, Harpreet, was sitting with the women at the far end of the lawn, on chairs that ringed a coal fire like a voodoo circle, heads straining inwards, the shadow of a conspiracy rising out of the fire as they measured against each other for all the things that their spouses did or did not do. They tapped into the passing spirits. A white-gloved waiter with his battered tray, both veterans of many a raucous party, was summoned quietly, with an inaudible psst. Double pegs of whisky sat in each of the glasses that trellised the tray. A quick spike in the cola, like a propitiation rite.

'He fights his sleep,' said Harpreet, 'like a baby.'

She had no idea why she was offering these confidences. She did not have to. The gathering was full of the diamond-clad. Diamonds were like regimental gear. You wore it, you were saluted. Harpreet never wore the right uniform. Her plain look was too severe for her surroundings. But confessionals were in the air like an infection.

The most resplendent of the women was now talking. 'Initially I was very upset and tried to make him break off with her. But he stuck to her like glue. She is not even nice looking. I decided that I might as well make myself happy. I just buy plenty of clothes and jewellery whenever I want and give him the bill. Every month I buy. Part of the monthly ration.'

'These men, I tell you, they are terrible.'

'It is only because of us women that marriages survive.'

Not all complaints were in the same league as a mistress in the closet though. There were also grumbles about the mundane. They ranged from the dripping wet bathroom that he left behind to the ill temper that accompanied even a mild fever to the fuss about food and the plateful of alu gobi flung against a wall, leaving behind a turmeric yellow bloom.

Harpreet added hers to the growing pile of grouses. 'The television in our bedroom is blaring all night. The minute I switch it off he wakes up.' It did not sound horrible enough even to her own ears, and she let it hang there unacknowledged.

She looked around and noticed the commotion near the stage. Craning her neck to try and spot the source of the disturbance she thought, we Punjabis love a good fight. A bam-bam fight in which there are a few displaced turbans and jaws and then everybody is ready for a good, hearty meal amidst a resurrected bonhomie, which is even more effusive after the battering it just suffered.

But then she spotted saffron at the centre of it all.

'I think that is your husband,' the resplendent one said to her.

'Don't worry,' said Mr Bakshi's daughter-in-law, Sarika. 'Harish is already there.'

Harish, her husband, had his arm around Tejpal and was walking him towards the house. 'Come. We will get a drink from the bar inside,' he said, removing Tejpal from the scene.

Balli hurried to catch up with them.

'Try taking deep breaths to soothe anger,' he said. 'It works like gargles. A nose-full of breath circles around in the brain, touching all the raw spots.'

Yet another diversion came by way of a recall.

'Oh! I nearly forgot. I had bought some cars today. I wonder if they were brought in,' said Harish, looking alternately green and red standing behind the counter of the bar, as the coloured lights that made up the canopy blinked in sequence. He spoke casually, as though he had picked up bags of peanuts and should have offered them earlier to his guests, to go with the drinks. No one was surprised at the absurdity of the purchase. He went out to check and came back to say, 'Want to come and see? I have asked them to bring the cars round to the front.'

In the driveway stood four diesel-run Mercedes.

'Mark my words,' said Harish, proudly eyeing his new acquisitions, 'ultimately we will all have to switch to diesel. Petrol prices will keep going up with these oil-rich mullahs dictating terms.'

'I should have been born an Arab sheikh. I wear a turban anyway. Could just as well have worn a flowing veil held in place by that ring. Much easier actually,' said Balli.

'You could also have had many wives. Expensive to keep them in good wifely humour though,' was Harish's response, though Balli had no wife at all.

With more money than he knew what to do with, Harish was always obsessive about its buying power.

The men walked around the cars, patted the bonnets, caressed the flanks, fiddled with the door handles, fussing over them like paranoid mothers.

In Ludhiana there were a couple hundred Mercedes plying the roads.

'How this town has changed from the little village it used to be when we were growing up,' Tejpal told Balli, his anger now merely winking bubbles after a smouldering effervescence.

He was not referring to Mir Hota, the village that it was in the sixteenth century when Sikandar Lodi's chief, Nihang Khan, settled in the region, patted it into shape and named it Lodiana. Tejpal was referring to the Ludhiana of the early sixties when cars did not sell like peanuts.

'We were idiots in our youth. We would chase after the occasional car on our street like village children, fascinated and amused by the urbanite and his gadgets.'

'I would even let out blood-curdling yells,' said Balli. He had used the Punjabi word badak to describe his cry—a cry which emanates from lips held loosely together and sounds like a challenge thrown to the world.

Tejpal continued to reminisce. 'Do you remember, on the other side of the Sirhind Canal there were only forests and witches and we had this crazy story about the baba with the long beard. It was so long that he tripped over it but became fleet-footed the minute he spied little children.'

'I think we had come up with that one only to discourage Kaka because we did not want him hanging around with us since he was too little to fit into our scheme of things. But

I had begun to believe my own stories about the baba and was quite scared myself.'

'So was I but I would have hated to admit it then.'

The forest had since disappeared. It was called South City now, and had rows of farmhouses equipped with their own golf courses and swimming pools.

Tejpal had been for a walk along the canal, hoping to resurrect some of the magic. The bushes that lined the canal on either side had looked menacing. That is where those witches came from, the ones with their feet turned inwards and their breasts so pendulous that they had to be thrown over their shoulders like a casual scarf. They would never have been able to walk if the twin udders had been allowed to hang loose in front. But he was not looking for witches or babas; he was looking for the sparkle from those days—the moon staring up at him from the water, surrounded by a protective army of a million stars. He would look up at the sky and expect it to have emptied, since the occupants had made their way down. And then he would be amazed at the endless supply up there.

✼

'Run, run. He is right behind you,' Tejpal would shout to Kaka.

Harish would offer practical advice, 'If he can't see you his beard will get entangled in his feet. Run so fast that he won't be able to see you.'

'Run, run Kaka. Disappear,' Balli would shout.

And all the while that they were urging Kaka on, they themselves were running that much faster, well ahead of Kaka, so that if the baba were to grab a tail, it would be Kaka and not them. Ultimately everyone would get away—

because childhood monsters are always much kinder than adult nightmares. It helps for monsters to have cumbersome breasts and overgrown beards.

In the harsh light of adulthood, the dusty walk along the canal had less romance and more discarded polythene bags. It did not look like the appropriate setting for mystery and adventure. The town itself was choking, houses following each other at a breathless pace to catch up on any gaps or open spaces, cars dovetailing into each other, motorcycles, scooters, rickshaws, autorickshaws, cycles and pedestrians crowding like an undifferentiated, crawling mass. The city had no lungs even for that occasional breath. But it was also said of the city that no one slept hungry here.

✖

In any case, no one at this party was likely to go to bed hungry unless liquor got the better of them. Most would make it to the dinner table around midnight. The guests had arrived only at about ten o'clock from a series of other parties and white-gloved waiters were plying them with food. You waved away one and another appeared almost at his heels. 'Fried fish,' he said. 'Chicken tikka,' said another. 'Mutton kabab'; 'French fries'; 'Honey-soaked cauliflower'. They were like persistent summer flies—the more you waved, the more they descended on you. Tejpal moved out of range of a proffered plate of tandoori paneer and asked Harish, 'Have you sold that house in Ghumar Mandi where we used to visit you?'

'Long ago,' said Harish.

As Mr Bakshi, Harish's father, had moved up the financial ladder, they had shifted house, changed furniture, acquired imported goods and altered their self-image. Mr Bakshi now stood tall, definitely taller than his five-feet-eight-inches, when he looked into the mirror.

Tejpal stuck a toothpick into a piece of boneless chicken, having succumbed to the onslaught of food, and asked Harish how they had managed when the Russians left the Ludhiana market.

'That was a tough phase but we changed our products and found other buyers,' said Harish, colouring a little with the blush of memories.

In Ludhiana there were many stories of new beginnings and dogged perseverance, of Kashmiri shawl-makers who came here during the 1840 famine in Kashmir and went on to create a carpet-making industry. Or the migrants of 1947 who started out by knitting socks on small machines installed in the house. Backyards would echo with the rat-a-tat sound of these machines—tak-tak-tak-tak-a-tak-tak. They went on to become exporters of hosiery, making huge sweaters with tea saucers as buttons, till the city came to be known as the Manchester of India. Tatters-to-tycoon stories. Russian buyers would arrive in large numbers, but housing them was a problem since the city had only two hotels. In the early sixties the hotels were always full of thickset Russian men and women with sturdy ankles descending into comfortable stomping shoes.

'How do you celebrate your birthdays if you don't drink vodka?' they had wonderingly asked Mr Bakshi over tea at his house.

'We eat pineapple pastries,' Mr Bakshi had told them. Gobind Sweets made them with a six-inch layer of shaving foam on top, designed to leave behind a white moustache of sweet stickiness.

Mr Bakshi's mother had told the Russians all about the missing carpets. And little Harish had pretended to be looking for his non-existent pencil by writhing around on the floor in the hope of catching a glimpse of what was under her skirt, never having seen a skirt, or for that matter what was under it, ever before in his life.

Then the USSR broke up and the Russians disappeared from the Ludhiana market. Harish had hoped that that would be the last he would hear of his juvenile endeavour to get under a skirt. However, Tejpal's reference to the Russians had been inadvertent and was not meant to be a wink and a nudge in the direction of skirts and what they veiled.

Just then the crackle of a mike coming alive drowned out all conversation.

'Hallo, hallo. One-two-three testing. One-two-three mike testing…' was followed by the sound of hammering, which was only the speaker drumming his fingernails on the mouthpiece and complaining, 'This is not working.' A fainter voice was heard telling him that it was and he only thought it was not working because the loudspeakers were placed at the far end of the lawn.

'Achha okay. Shall I begin?'

The speaker began again, but this time in his mike-worthy voice.

'Ladies and gentlemen, please come to the drawing room,' said the voice. 'The ceremonies are about to begin.'

It took several more announcements along the same line—with the voice on the mike going from measured, deep and cadenced, to desperate, screeching and persistent—to dislodge people from their groups and propel them in the desired direction.

He varied his calls.

'Please come, one and all,' he said, taking his cue from the announcements that he made for Saturday tambola at the club and at the annual fair.

'Come one. Come all.'

'Come and get your seats in the front row for the big event.'

The event was the release of Mr Bakshi's book. He had hired a scribe to ghostwrite the story of his life. It had been difficult to find somebody to perform the onerous task since the job required skill in rhetoric and bombast.

'I knew in my heart that I could climb the highest mountains and reach the peak to plant the flag of my victory. It is my strength of character that has made me what I am. I buffeted the storms of my life with a determined mind and heart. Each step was a struggle. But at every step there was achievement. So, step by step my journey went on. And now, I am plucking the fruits of my effort...' There was this and lots more of the same.

Dictation mornings were an arduous affair for the scribe. Mr Bakshi would push his chair away from the desk, lean it backwards, stretch his legs out in front of him, clasp his hands behind his head and stare at the ceiling for inspiration. The lone lizard in the corner would become self-conscious and scurry away on little legs; an eavesdropper in its last life, it had to be a lizard in this one with its ear to the wall. The scribe would doodle in the margins of the page and wait.

Mr Bakshi would say, 'My life has been such a success'— and complete the sentiment with a sigh of satisfaction. The scribe would write down the sentence. Other times Mr Bakshi would rattle off chronological details of births and deaths within the family or in his social circle. He had no doubt about their historical significance or of his own important place in the march of time. Meanwhile, the scribe would be rummaging through his head for flowery figures of speech, for sentences that would curl into pretty daisies at the end.

The Story of My Life was to be an inspiring account of Mr Bakshi's life, and everything one wanted to know about starting afresh. It worked like a hot-air pump on his ego, sending him floating above the skyline. However, shorn of all the self-congratulation, it was an honest account of his life. Though the book left everyone, or at least those who rifled through it, wishing that he had pretended some humility, even if he felt none.

It was a coffee table edition, with Mr Bakshi staring out of coloured photographs. 'Mr Bakshi enjoying in a swimming pool', 'Mr Bakshi enjoying on the streets of London', 'Mr Bakshi in different moods' said the lucid captions. Occasionally, in a burst of generosity, the book conceded print space to other members of his family and towards featuring his houses. The books sat in enormous piles on a glass table in the centre of the drawing room. On the lower shelf of the table a number of magazines lay casually strewn around. These were usually bought by Mrs Bakshi through the window of her car. She would roll down the window when the car came abreast of the magazine vendor's stand, and ask for a few glossy periodicals.

'Give me ten,' she would say. 'Preferably imported. I have a party tonight.'

But these magazines were obscured today, their pride of place having been taken by the home production. The guests were each going to get a return gift—their own prized copy of the first edition of this glorified family album.

Mr Bakshi gave a speech.

'Ladies and gentlemen,' he said, with the flourish of a man who had finally got hold of the mike and did not intend relinquishing it without a fight. 'Let me start the ball rolling, as they say in cricket, and tell you all about my life. Let me be frank with you: I came here with nothing, litter-ly nothing, and now you all know what respect I enjoy in this town. Last year the Global Punjabi Conference called me. I was given a very befitting honour. Some of you have been to my office, no? There you must have seen my photographs with prime ministers, presidents and so many other important people. And now those pictures will be with you in this book. Thanks God that I have been so successful. But mind it, it is not without hard work.'

He was right though. Behind the ornate office chair in which he sat was a wall of photographs of himself: receiving a gift, receiving an award, giving away a gift, giving an award, snipping an inaugural ribbon, standing in a group with a bunch of somebodies.

'I was in Rawalpindi when Partition took place. And as I was telling Tejpal here, we were in great danger there when the riots began. I got away from there in a truck. My entire family came here that way. We all—my family, my father, my brother and sister—we lived in a huge haveli in Rawalpindi.'

He took advantage of the liberty that is available to the migrant to assume an identity and a past. If he had said that they once ate out of gold plates studded with diamonds and embossed with their own coat of arms, there was no way of verifying it, their past having been left behind in another country. So a mansion it was.

'We lived in a haveli,' he said. 'It was known as "Bakshian

di haveli", a landmark, and people pointed to it as they went past. My father was in the trading business.'

There were not many in the audience who were interested in Mr Bakshi, and even less so in his father. But then, he had the mike. A microphone in the hand makes the audience irrelevant and the speaker self-sufficient. He hears only his own voice as it comes back to him magnified, laden with its own echoes. He does not hear the disinterested buzz of conversation, the desultory applause, the unsaid 'boo'.

'He, my father, was a very respected man in society. Any important function in town was not complete without him. Even Englishmen came to take advice from him. To be very frank with you, when we left and came here in August 1947, we came with nothing. It was August twelve, I still remember. It was raining so much all the way that even my underwear was also soaked. We came to the Jawahar Refugee Camp here. The government gave us money every month to live. Three years we lived like that only. Then the government decided that families with men must earn themselves. They started giving us less money. So we came to Model Town and rented a room. To be very frank with you, we all lived in that one room. You see my house now,' he said, waving his arms expansively to encompass it all—the house, the chandeliers, the minarets, the domes, the gardens. 'And you will not believe that at one time my father did not have thirteen annas to send me to school beyond class seven.'

He repeated the last sentence to emphasize the enormity of it all.

'He did not have thirteen annas to send me to school!'

'Thirteen annas!' he said again, like a rendition in Indian classical music in which the artist improvises a threefold repetitive musical sequence.

'You will not believe that I sold peanuts from a rehri and even went from house to house selling newspapers early in the morning, before going to school. And see how successful I have been. I wish my father was here to see me today. He would have been a proud man. Apart from making a flourishing business, I have now also written a book. The area from where I come, Pothohar, which is now in Pakistan, is known for its literary people. All literary people in English literature or Punjabi literature come from Pothohar.'

He proceeded to list all the biggies of the industry and established for himself an exalted literary lineage. 'And now, not the least, myself.'

The gathering was beginning to lose patience with the Bakshi saga. The clusters standing right in front of him found it difficult to move, pinned to their place by the Bakshi eye. He was addressing them directly. They looked around shiftily, trying to avoid direct eye contact while rapidly sipping their drinks, parched sponges into which whole glassfuls disappeared; hoping to project their hurry on to the speaker. The rest of the party was discreetly becoming vapour. By the time Mr Bakshi held up his book to indicate its release, since he was doing the honours himself, the flashbulbs of hired cameras exploded but the backbenchers had already bolted. The loudspeakers burst into song:

Congratulations and celebrations
When I tell everyone that you're in love with me.

The DJ had selected the song with an eye on the first line.

At the far end of the room, conversation was in full flow, unmindful of the passion and perseverance of the speaker. Balli was saying to Tejpal, 'A Singh after all! You had to land up in the wrong place at the wrong time.' He was attempting to cheer Tejpal by drawing on the self-deprecating humour of the Sikh community. 'You heard about the Singh in Kerala. There was a fire in a tea factory and while everyone else was running away from it, he was running towards it. And I am not joking. Even the papers, *Malayala Manorama* it was, carried a story about him. H. M. S. Pannu, I think his name was, and he was running towards this raging fire in the hope of rescuing some documents,' said Balli.

Tejpal laughed. 'And why not Santa Singh or Banta Singh who are the regulars in Surdi jokes? Why H. M. S. Pannu, like a ship?'

'You think I am joking? You think I have cooked up the name, dreamt it up?' protested Balli. 'This one is for real.'

But all Tejpal dreamt of was marauding hordes. He was running... Always running. Breathless but running. Panting and running. Wheezing and running. Terrified and running. But the futility of action in dreams made escape impossible. The mob always caught up with him.

'Try using a car in your dream,' Balli said to him. 'Maybe you can ask Harish to park one of his new Mercedes' there.'

'Won't work,' said Tejpal, warming up to the image. 'It will involve too much reversing and changing of gears.'

✖

He would be running for miles through little lanes and by-lanes and each time he would emerge at the same square. By then, the crowd bearing down on him would have inched still closer at each successive appearance. He would turn around and run. The background score in all his dreams would be a combination of a drum beating time to a marching drill and the steadily heightening roar of a mob on rampage. Looking back down the length of the road he had run, he would see a tea shop where a huge aluminium teapot sat on a clay oven, in which the flames just kept rising higher and higher till they were slurping on the leaves of the tree overhead.

The large clay oven, the tandoor at Mr Bakshi's party, had grilling rods standing in it, strung with chunks of cottage cheese and pieces of onion and capsicum like gigantic emerald and moonstone necklaces. The tandoor stood in one corner of the lawn where a few of the more adventurous women had strayed with their dinner plates. Among them was Harpreet. There was talk of designer clothes and the futility of buying them in Ludhiana, since that would compromise their exclusivity.

'Every party you go to, somebody is bound to be wearing the same clothes as you,' lamented one.

'I always buy my clothes in Delhi or in London when we are there,' said another.

There were also philosophical observations about simple living and high thinking. This had come from Sarika, the gold bangles on her arm jangling, the diamonds on her finger emitting sparks, as she declared the motto of her life. It was unclear how she would achieve it in the plenty of her surroundings. In fact, her brand new diamond ring just happened to be visible in each photograph that featured her. No happy coincidence that! (Post-party photograph browsing revealed that she was wearing it alternately on both hands, keeping a careful eye on the hand that was likely to be exposed to the camera.)

Harpreet wandered off to look for Tejpal in a preliminary move to leave for home.

Tejpal resisted. He always did. It was part of his epic battle against sleep. First he would cling to his glass. Then he would linger over his food. Once home, he would put off the evil moment of getting into bed till sleep overcame him on the sofa in front of the television. His head would droop as though attached to his torso by a particularly tensile rubber tube.

He had to keep awake because the moment he would fall asleep he would step right into the sword-wielding crowd that he had been trying to dodge the night before.

✴

This headlong plunge into trouble in his dream had to do with that November morning of 1984 when, clad in his red turban, he had stretched, yawned and stepped off the train on to the railway platform at Old Delhi station, at a time when everyone else with the burden of a turban was trying to hide. But he had had absolutely no idea about this. He was fresh with the innocence of a sound sleep that had been induced by the gentle rocking of the train. Newspapers were told to blank out news of the violence that came on the heels of the assassination of the prime minister. There were blank spaces in newspaper columns with 'Censored' boldly written across. Behind the words that were never written were stories of mass killing and looting. But Tejpal did not know.

The morning before, he had been standing outside a government office in Chandigarh for an eleven o'clock meeting where he was to be evaluated for the grant of a loan of six lakhs. This was seed capital for first-generation entrepreneurs.

He wanted to start a factory and already had his patch of land on the outskirts of Chandigarh. He had been through a series of interviews to qualify for this final one.

But the government office was strangely quiet and empty on what should have been a working day. Officialdom has its own rhythm of laxity and activity, he thought with resignation.

'Someone will show up some time,' he assured himself.

'What's going on?' he asked a uniformed peon who had sauntered in, seated himself on a bench, kicked off one shoe and folded his leg under him.

'Go home,' he said. 'Nothing is going to happen today. In fact, nothing at all is going to happen for many days. Indira has been shot dead.' He was referring to the prime minister of the country, but he spoke of her as though they had been on first-name terms.

Tejpal looked blank.

'Who?' he asked, his mind still preoccupied with the possible outcome of the forthcoming interview and visions of the factory that was already going up brick by brick in his mind's eye.

'Indira. Indira Gandhi. You don't know her?' the peon said with impatience.

'Oh, I thought you were referring to somebody in this office,' Tejpal replied lamely.

'No, no. I am talking of Indira. I know she is dead, though All India Radio is trying to pretend she is not.'

It was a first-name familiarity born of heated political discussions amongst the peon and his friends as they sat awaiting the next bidding from their bosses in the secretariat. Political bigwigs were household names.

'Rajiv broke down and cried,' he added. He had perfected

the art of adding just that little bit of home-grown spice that would remain within the realm of the credible but would give him an edge over the others. 'Saab was here but he went home to listen to the news. You better come after a week or so. No one will be working here for the next few days.'

He should know what he is talking about, thought Tejpal, given the fact that a bench outside an office is a vantage point. In any case, Tejpal was booked on the Kalka Mail that left Chandigarh at midnight and arrived in Delhi at daybreak. A brief halt at his camp office there, a bath and breakfast and then he would board the train to Gwalior. It was a journey he had taken many times over, ever since he decided to set up his own outfit, having worked as the manager of a factory in Gwalior. He walked out to his waiting cab and directed the driver to the site for his factory.

The land had been purchased many years ago. The to-buy-or-not-to-buy debate had closed with his father's conclusive remark: 'Beta, God has stopped making more earth.'

Any piece of land was therefore bound to become more valuable with time. Tejpal spent the afternoon tending to the saplings that he had planted there. The seed capital for the factory would, however, have to wait.

By evening he was back at the railway station. He spread his bedding in the single coach to Delhi that waited on the tracks for the rest of the train from Kalka, and went to sleep, his body still warm from the afternoon sun and tired from the exertions of the day.

The Chandigarh railway station did not offer much by way of activity—two desultory bookstalls, a loud chorus of birds chirruping in the overhead rafters, bird shit that came flying through the air and had to be dodged, a few tired boxes sitting on the platform waiting to be loaded. It was a good place to catch up on any appointments that one had with oneself. Tejpal usually caught up with missed sleep on this leg of his journey. He did not hear the Kalka Mail arrive nor did he feel the shudder when his coach was attached to it. When he woke up, the train had just reached Delhi and he cheerfully stepped on to the platform, bag in hand.

At the wrong place, at the wrong time.

2

Jasmer Kaur's house was an anachronism in time. There was an endless brick path from the gate to the house. A field of matted weeds threatened to swamp the path. A forest of fruit trees shaded it. The house had a cantankerous bell that rang only sometimes, after repeated jabs at it. The noise of the traffic outside was a muted murmur. And growing old with her house, her wrinkled hands now matching the knots in the barks of the trees, her chin sprouting unwanted hair like weeds, Jasmer Kaurhad become 'aunty' for the English speaking and 'mataji' or 'beeji' for the hawkers with their pushcarts full of vegetables. But she had been Jassi when she was young and she continued to think of herself as Jassi.

The gentle tinkle of a spoon in her afternoon cup of tea was suddenly interrupted by Kailla's rant. 'Kaille da kalesh', she called it. It had to have a name because it had become institutionalized. It happened every day.

'Just you wait. I am coming,' he was shouting to the children who had crept in to steal the fruit and to seek entertainment in the chase that inevitably followed, in which they were always at an advantage. Kailla hobbled along behind them. He was a wiry man with eyes that started out of his head. The clumsy swirls of his turban usually came unstuck the minute he moved. The bottoms of his pyjama flapped as he hastened after them.

'You just stand right there. I am coming to get you,' he said, trying to tuck in the loose ends of his turban while negotiating his walk, both at the same time. There was hardly any likelihood of the children waiting around to be thrashed. They sped away shouting out to him, 'Chacha, we will see you tomorrow. Can't wait just now. Have business to attend to. We are in a hurry.'

'Just you wait,' he shouted. 'I will watch out for you tomorrow and then you won't get away.'

Kailla lived in the outhouse from where he kept one sleeping ear cocked for the giggles of the children creeping in. He even went through the ritual of locking the gate every afternoon, but the younger ones climbed over the barrier and the older ones vaulted over it.

When he was younger, he could occasionally catch one or two of them. He would raise his hand and threaten them with dire consequences, but all he did was give them a vigorous shaking. He grew old but the children remained young, one generation having handed the baton to the next, passing on information of a house with lots of trees loaded with fruit, of a man who merely shouted, gave ineffective chase and threatened but did not beat, of a kind-looking woman in the house whose face appeared at the window sometimes but who did not say anything.

Jassi had been averse to renting out her annex to young couples because the one time that she had, the experience had been surreal. She would be drifting into the sweat-drenched sleep of a summer afternoon when her half-awake mind would catch the sounds of a violent quarrel. She would look out of the window, and her tenant, a tough young woman, would be dragging her husband by his hair and appealing to the world for justice. A Sikh in a physical fight is always at a disadvantage since the turban is easily toppled and the long hair unfurling from under is a proffered weapon, handle first. The young wife invariably made a grab for it. The few times that Jassi had stepped out, she had been asked to 'look, *look* at the wretched man'. She had never been able to understand what to look for and just what was so evil about the man who was being dragged by his hair, other than the wretchedness of being dragged by the hair. She had decided then not to risk young couples and their raw emotions.

However, the first impression that she had of this other couple, who had been in her annex for about ten years now, was that they held together; and though they seemed to carry around some sort of a burning ember, it was so deep within them that it was not likely to spark into a display of pyrotechnics down the drive. Besides, they had come here after the anti-Sikh riots of 1984, and that resonated in her being. Even now, when she reached deep inside, there was a point that hurt dully.

The morning after Tejpal and Harpreet had settled in, the children spotted a new face at the window when they were hoisting themselves on to the gate. Should they go in? The split second of indecision was, however, automatically resolved in favour of a halla bol, a continued charge, since the momentum that carried them to the top of the gate also deposited them at the bottom on the other side. They barely had time to make it to the trees and Kailla was already out, shouting his lines: 'You just wait. I am coming.'

Harpreet was watching from the window of the annex, and Jassi from hers. Too many people, thought the children, and ran for it with Kailla in hot pursuit.

Harpreet had laughingly called out to Kailla, 'Why don't you let the children eat some of this overload on the trees? I am sure Jassi would not mind.'

That one sentence had won Jassi over—she herself kept telling Kailla to let the children be. It suggested a sense of belonging, as though Harpreet were already a part of the household. Also, she liked being called Jassi. That was the beginning of their friendship.

The day after the party Harpreet wiped the sweat from Tejpal's brow and said, 'Why are you sweating?'

A sleeping Tejpal was always more lovable than Tejpal awake. She would watch him negotiate his breath between snores and feel the urge to soothe him.

'Because I ran,' he said. 'Because I ran, like a mouse,' he repeated.

It was exhausting. He had to run even in his sleep, overpowered by the slow viscousness of dreams, by the inabilities that crowd them—the examination hall that cannot be reached as time ticks away and you stand in your underwear unable to find the right clothes, or the pen that refuses to write at the last minute. But Tejpal's dream was a labyrinth without an exit, peopled with a mob that sounded like a congregation of flies in conversation.

✱

He had stepped off the train at the Old Delhi Railway Station in his red turban. There was a press of cabbies vying to relieve him of his bag and herd him to their taxis. He had instinctively picked one with a red turban.

'Where to, sardarji?' asked the taxi driver.

'Janakpuri,' he said, which was where his company had a branch office.

It was very early in the morning. On the way there was a campfire in the middle of the road. Or so it seemed. Furniture was piled up twenty feet high and was burning rapidly.Black smoke curled into the white, wispy clouds in the sky, dirtying them.

'Some sort of clearing up?' he asked the driver.

'This is a rowdy area. Lots of gundagardi. Could be anything.'

'Even if they are only trying to warm up a cold November morning, why in the middle of the road?'

As they skirted the volcanic mountain of furniture, they saw a human leg sticking out from the bottom of the heap.

'Told you this was a bad area,' said the taxi driver.

They shuddered and drove past. Amidst the smell of burning wood, a fleeting smell, quickly submerged, of burning flesh. A sudden waft again and then they had moved on.

Tejpal washed and bathed in the camp office, then read the paper, which was inked black with news of the prime minister's assassination by her Sikh bodyguards. He contemplated awhile on how the commonplace eludes extraordinary lives even in death. Dying in bed of old age would be far too tame an end for the daughter of the first prime minister of independent India. But he had never liked her and could not say that he was sorry. There was something to be said for a life that was routine. You wake up in the morning and go to bed at night. At least no one thinks of gunning you down. Amidst such philosophical thoughts on the ironies of life he called for a cab to take him to the station to catch the eleven-thirty to Gwalior. 'Come and get it,' each of the drivers said, when he sent his office peon to the taxi stand. None would come to the building. He was surprised at the sudden intransigence of taxi drivers. He walked to the stand, carrying his overnight bag, the picture of normality beginning to curl at the edges.

A busload of ruffians went by.

'Sardar, sardar, maro, maro, kill him, kill him,' they shouted, pointing to him.

He gawked. Just when he had thought the ordinariness of his life was his armour. They could not be serious. They were just a bunch of hooligans getting a laugh out of the stupid look on his face. He waited for the bus to be on its way. But it stopped. And then they were streaming out, armed with clubs and swords.

'Maro, maro.'

There was an explosion of blood inside his head. He scurried into a by-lane and ran wildly. Like a mouse, he thought. He did not look back as that would have slowed him down, but concentrated instead, on getting away from the hungry-eyed mob. That was the stuff his subsequent dreams were made of: the maniacal running, the attempt to keep his feet quiet even as he ran, willing them to fall softly on the tarmac, hiding behind doorways, cautiously peeping round a corner before plunging on.

He had run through a number of by-lanes when he finally felt he had outrun danger. In the distance he saw a small dhaba at the foot of an ancient banyan tree. An old sardar with a flowing white beard was kindling a tandoor, putting small pieces of wood into it and occasionally stirring its depths with a fireiron. Tejpal waited for the heavy pounding of his heart to subside, for his legs to solidify once again into bone and muscle before he made his way there. The sardar was a kindly looking old man. Maybe it was the sudden antithesis he offered, but even now Tejpal thought of him as the most handsome man ever. He went up to him and asked for some tea.

'Babaji, how long have you been running this place?' He was making small talk as the nearly viscous mixture of water, milk, sugar and tea leaves gurgled in the weather-beaten pot, reassuring himself that the ordinariness of life was still intact.

'Been over forty years now,' said the old man as he poured the contents of the pot into a glass through a tea-blackened sieve.

Tejpal rubbed his hands together in anticipation of tea and also as a closure to the cat-and-mouse game. He had just curled his cold fingers around the hot glass of tea when the mob appeared around the corner once again. He thumped his glass down on the table. The tea sloshed all over his hand, scalding it, but he ran.

As he looked back from the head of the lane, he saw that the mob had caught hold of the old man and was swinging him into the fire. That is where his visual frame froze forever.

✹

When Harpreet wiped the sweat from his brow, he had woken up mid-stride. But he had also left behind an old man being roasted in an oven. And now that he was awake, he could not alter anything.

✹

Tejpal had been to a school in Ludhiana where most of his class fellows were sons of industrialists—some petty, some giants.

His father was a people person, prone to unleashing practical jokes. His favourite one was from the time when India had neither independence from the British nor a national anthem. He was enrolled in an engineering course in London and when students from different nations were asked to sing their anthems he had gone on to sing a Punjabi folk song; standing at attention, hand on his heart and a grave look on his face, though he was singing about a wily old traveller who stopped for a night at a lodging run by a woman and left behind two counterfeit annas as payment after availing of everything she had to offer. 'Everything' was a matter of speculation and could be stretched as far as the imagination would go.

'*Nalle baba raat reh gaya, nalle de gaya doanni khoti,*' he sang.

The assembly of European students stood straight and stiff, whilst laughter gurgled silently in his chest.

To Tejpal he would describe the time, back in 1915, when he and others would meet at the Dewa Singh Sports Goods shop in Chaura Bazaar. His narratives usually came with appropriate sound effects. He could never mention the word motorcycle without an accompanying, prolonged 'zoooooo' which went from a low note to a high-pitched one, or a resounding slap that was always a 'phataak'. There were many others and the accounts always became a dramatic enactment. Tejpal's father's stories were foggy and exciting. Tejpal never understood everything.

'We would usually gather at the sports shop because we had to each collect our share of the pamphlets that were to be distributed. We would talk in whispers. Phus phus...phus phus. Not that it made any difference because we kept getting into trouble anyway. We would keep telling each other to shhh up because that had been our problem. We could never keep a secret. The angrez always knew in advance what we were going to do next.'

'Did they know you?'

'No. They just knew us as the ghaddaris—rebels. They also knew that in the February of 1915, we were all going to rebel against the British. I was very little then, only good for fetching and carrying. And that is what I did. But the others, the older boys, had plans. They were going to destroy railway stations and police posts, disable post and telegraph systems, cause disarray in military camps and set up their own camps in jungles and border areas.'

'But I am sure the angrez knew you were one of the rebels. They must have been afraid of you.' Tejpal could not imagine anyone not knowing his father.

'We had just picked up a handful of those pamphlets and were headed out of the shop when one of those English policemen gave us chase. We barely made it because my friend dropped some leaflets and stopped to gather them, and I had to run back and help him.'

And then in a philosophical tone, he added, 'Bravery came so easily those days. It was fuelled by a righteous anger and we would just surge ahead on its torrential flow.'

✶

When Tejpal finally drove into Ludhiana on that cold November morning of 1984, after a journey on the razor's edge, he felt nothing, not even anger. After he escaped from the mob he had been refused help by a senior police official who had told him he was on his own. Terrified, he had hidden on rooftops, and had watched two Sikh men being hurled off a neighbouring roof. He had been partially reassured when he found shelter with a friend; and had finally dumped his pride and identity and removed his turban, taken his hair down, smeared his forehead with a red tikka, and become Swami Vidhi Chand. His friend did not recognize him as he held up his hand in blessing. 'Tathaastu,' he said, and his friends gawked at this apparition that appeared to have fallen in through the roof. It was in this guise that he had travelled to Gwalior, only to find that he and his wife had to flee from there as well, because the mob had names and addresses there, too, and were carefully, methodically, going from one house to the other, making sure to kill, burn and loot.

All through the drive his wife sat beside him. Two large suitcases were thrown carelessly into the boot of his car along with a random selection of household goods—cushions, crockery, cutlery, gadgets, linen. There had been no time for considered choices. A hasty inventory made in a fleeting glance, things picked only because they were closest at hand, a moment of indecision between two necessities resolved in passing; racing against the crowd that was even now arming itself with swords and petrol somewhere in town.

The baggage in the boot, the car that they drove and a healthy bank balance were all that he had to show for all those years spent as a busy executive. He had arrived in Ludhiana with a frown wrinkling his forehead, eyes shadowed under by sleeplessness, worry lines creasing the rest of his face, his chin firmly set, not in any display of determination but more from the emotional necessity of gritting his teeth. Arriving at midnight, they had parked their car in front of the gurdwara at Kichlew Nagar. The familiar sight of a gurdwara, any gurdwara, offered a feeling of relief which had nothing to do with religion. It just gave them a sudden sense of belonging.

The town was characterized by frenzied industrial activity with neither time nor breathing space for any ghosts, nor for any finer sentiments that might pass for culture. Tejpal had parked here quite instinctively because this was where his parents had lived in later years after his father's retirement from the Punjab Agricultural University and before their deaths. Harpreet and he had looked at each other and cried silently for a few minutes in homage to their lost lives. Before this, there had been no time to cry. They had then debated waking some friends to find a bed for the night but decided against it. Neither of them had the emotional energy to give a coherent account of the events to anyone, least of all to those who would wake up from sleep—those whose lives were still determined by the certainties of the everyday.

'We will just sleep in the car,' was all they said to each other, hoping that the morning would look different. And it did. They had woken up in the early hours and already the streets were beginning to fill up with traffic, the silence of the night broken by milk delivery men on motorcycles, the tinkling of cycle bells as labourers on early morning shifts made their way to their workplaces.

Once the immediate sense of danger diminished, Harpreet began to feel that there had been something strangely unfettered about their journey. Just a road ahead and they could have gone anywhere, any milestones past any green fields. But they had driven into Ludhiana.

The first settlers, the no-baggage itinerants, the Rajputs and later the Jats wandering in from the South, must have looked at the Sutlej river and said, 'Here is where we stop,' and may have gone on to say, 'we may as well put down our backpacks and seek permission from whomever it is that gives permission.' And no matter how dusty and tired those first settlers must have been, they had made an epic journey. The kind that creates castles out of thin air; when the dust clears, a whole city is in place.

Some said Ludhiana took its name from the Lodhi dynasty in the fifteenth century; others believed it dated back to many thousand years before Christ, during the time of the Vedas. But the romance of antiquity was soon submerged by the scramble for existence.

Into this city Tejpal and Harpreet had come, the skyline teeming with rooftops as far as the eye could see. They had been welcomed into Harish's house. His father, the honourable Mr Bakshi, had lectured them on the mettle it takes to begin again.

'Look at me,' he said. 'You will not believe that I started with nothing, just like you will have to today. Of course, it is not everyone who can do it. You have to be very determined.'

3

Tejpal's friend Balli had a problem. He did not know he had one though. Too much had happened between the genesis of the problem and its manifestation.

'She is like my sister,' he would say. That applied to all the women he knew as well as to the millions he did not. Perhaps the sentiment had been reinforced by his parents, who were always describing each little girl who visited their house—a friend's daughter, the housemaid's daughter, the pigtailed girl in his class whom he was great friends with—as 'your sister'. But then this was no different from most parents who unconsciously hope to put off the evil moment of the discovery of sexuality in their children. Balli had taken it to heart.

On rakhi day he would have an armful of rakhis, all the way up from his wrist to his elbow, each the size of a big dahlia that had to be tied at a breathing distance from yet another blooming flower. Some featured a layer of tissue over a petal-shaped sponge, a bulbous daisy with a silver butterfly in the centre, others were a flurry of gold and silver tinsel with red velvet shapes spreading amoeba-like on the arm. A whole line-up of these, from his tiny wrist to his bony elbow, professing sisterly affection, were secured to his arm by little girls. The thread of love seemed to have tied him in knots.

'They are not your sisters really,' Tejpal and Harish protested.

'But they are like my sisters.'

Oldest ploy in the book, this one. Boys in school would say this to worm their way closer to the girls, and film stars in Bombay modified it a little to 'we're just good friends' and used it as a cover-up for relationships.

What made Balli's case different was that he was entirely serious about his peculiar angle on one half of the population. Not quite half though, since the population in Punjab has a skewed sex ratio. Part of the responsibility for this rested with his ancestors from the nineteenth century, who would put a piece of molasses in the mouth of a baby girl and a skein of cotton on her breast, and chant as they put her in a water pot and buried her in the ground.

Eat molasses,
Spin your thread!
We don't want you
But a brother instead.

Balli moved on from those big orbs on his right arm to sober, single threads in college and onto a bachelorhood that was teetering on the edge of perpetuity. His father had not given up though.

'Maybe you can convince Balli to get married,' said his father to Tejpal. 'We have a girl in mind, but Balli refuses to go and meet her.'

Actually there was a range on offer for selection. There were four daughters in that household, each born within a year of the other, and Balli had been offered the pick of the lot. They also had plenty of money thanks to a massive slice of land that the family owned in the heart of Ludhiana. Land prices had gone up a near vertical gradient and all they had to do was sell a few crumbs that fell from the table and that would be enough to marry the girls. Enough to buy a marriage outfit at the price of a car, a car at the price of an aeroplane and a house at the price of a trip to the moon.

Balli decided to go and see the girls because he had been toying with the idea of getting married. The added impetus was that Tejpal and Harpreet had agreed to accompany him and his father. His mother was a ghostly presence, a sighing shadow that floated in and exhaled the chill of some deep-seated sentiment and sailed out. It was only occasionally that she participated.

'Shall we go?' Balli's father emerged from his room all trussed up, his pink turban matching the pink shirt under his coat.

'Let's,' said Balli without enthusiasm.

'And don't ask the girls to tie a rakhi on your wrist,' Tejpal advised him.

The house of the prospective brides was a series of sitting rooms. At the entrance two chairs flanked a carved wooden table, followed by a lobby with a flowery sofa set, an atrium with a leafy roof and garden chairs and then the drawing room. Traversing through the endless sitting spaces, Harpreet wondered if they had any bedrooms at all.

'Which one?' Balli's father whispered to him after the preliminaries. He was referring to the four girls and not the numerous drawing rooms. They had been ushered into the room reserved for the most important events.

Balli shifted nervously on the velvet sofa and carefully examined his shoes, which were black and shining. He even leaned over and dusted off a speck with the paper napkin he was holding in his hand. It was attention to detail in the hope that the larger picture would disappear in a poof, leaving only him and his black shoes.

He looked up to see that the girls were floating clouds of gossamer veils in different colours. The centre table was burdened with sweets of all kinds. Orange jalebis, barfi glistening with silver foil, gulab jamuns soaked in syrup, a darkly brown chocolate cake, sandwiches, cutlets. It was difficult to choose.

'Try some,' the girls said to Balli, holding out each of the dishes in turn.

'Which one?' said his father.

'*Akkad bakkad bambe bo, assi nabbe poore sau, sau kalota titar mota, chal madari paisa khota.*'

The elimination count went through Balli's head, the jabbing finger of his mind going from one girl to the other. And wherever it stopped at 'paisa khota', which in any case meant a dud coin, that girl was out and he could then start with the remaining players. It was only a game in his head and not meant to operate as the decider because he was already beginning to feel fraternal towards the girls. But the timing of his father's query happened to coincide with the conclusion to the counting rhythm in his head and the jabbing finger turned into an inordinately long wooden pointer. It was the pointer that his geography teacher wielded when she stood aside from the board to give her students a clear view of the map, and traced the journey of the river Sutlej in its westward drift, explaining Ferrel's law to them. But Ferrel's law was only black lines with arrows, capturing neither the personality of the river nor the drama of the journey. And he liked to think of the river as a horse in full gallop.

Just when the geography teacher's pointer had wended its way in and around the districts of Ropar, Samrala and Jagraon and had arrived at a confluence with the other galloping River Beas at Harike, Balli's jabbing finger declared Girl Number Two as the winner. His father chose that moment to pop the question to him once again. 'Which one?' he said, and this time it was louder, almost a stage whisper. Without realizing it, Balli's flesh and blood finger pointed to Girl Number Two though he was merely indicating the winner of the last elimination round and not his choice.

But the place erupted into an explosion of celebration before he could contain his finger. 'Mubarkan, mubarkan, congratulations, congratulations'—they all said to each other. It all happened so quickly but in his mind it was a slow dance of deliberate actions, of people hugging each other and offering the silver-foiled barfi, clicking photographs of Girl Number Two and him seated side by side on the velvet sofa, feeding each other a piece of barfi, standing with her parents, then his father, then with Tejpal and Harpreet. They gave him five gold coins as an initial offering, sealing the contract to marry. *We put our money down on you.*

The other girls had now melted into the background like participants at a beauty contest who had recited their lines for the camera and were now gradually bowing their way out. The moving finger writes, he thought, and having writ, moves on.

The journey back was a sombre affair. He did not want to get married.

He examined various excuses to call off the engagement. Should he tell his father that he had a girlfriend? But then he would be required to produce her immediately with the added responsibility of explaining why he had kept her hidden all this while. Nor would it mitigate his crime if attention were drawn to the fact that his father had bought a woman for rupees five hundred in the hilly resort of Manali, way back in the early fifties, and had kept her there for many years, hidden from everyone. His mother's occasional remarks about the uncertainty of her own status within this house, and the angrily spat out words—'that woman!', told him that it was not just rumour. Maybe some of her sighs took their chill from the cold in Manali, from the snows that capped the mountains that surrounded it.

But the only girls Balli knew were either his rakhi sisters or his friends' wives.

He could also say that he was impotent, which he well might be, given the fact that he continued to be in a state of blessed virginity. But impotence was an excuse that girls used to annul marriages that they wanted to wish away, and it seemed like self-flagellation to be accusing himself of impotence. Besides, it would put the shadow of unmanliness on him and he may just as well have said that he was a homosexual. So, he resorted to the ridiculous. It was only meant to be a facetious attempt at putting off the wedding and he wanted to see just how far things could be stretched.

'The girl's teeth were not well aligned,' he told his father.

'Her teeth!' he said. 'How did you get to see her teeth?'

'She smiled, didn't she?'

'Whom was she smiling at? I did not see you smiling even once. In fact, you looked grim enough to be at a funeral.'

'I was coping as best I could. I did not think there was anything to smile about.'

He had not expected his father to do what he did next. His father could be brash, aggressive and loud, the kind who could embarrass you in a restaurant (such that when Balli was a teenager, he would usually act as though he had no idea how this gentleman with the booming voice happened to be sitting at the same table as him). Yet he did not expect this.

As soon as his back was turned, his father rang up the household with the four daughters.

'My son thinks that the girl has crooked teeth.'

'That is no matter at all. This is your house. You are welcome any time. Come again and see for yourself,' said her father.

The offer was actually taken up by Balli's father, who discreetly made a second visit to their house. When told of the event, after his father made a triumphant return home, Balli squirmed each time he tried to reconstruct the scene. Before leaving for the house his father must have had his usual ten-towel bath—one for his hair, one for his face, one for his torso, one for his back, one for his underarms, one for his upper limbs, one for his lower limbs, one for his genitals, one for his feet and one for wrapping around his middle as he stepped out of his bathroom into the dressing room. This was not from a neurotic disorder but from a desire to luxuriate in excess, whether it be towels or turbans. His father must have pulled out his brightest shirt and carried it to a cupboard full of turbans. He must have run the shirt across all these like a shopkeeper trying to match a sari blouse, located the best approximation, and then proceeded to get ready. He must have left the house with a strut, his moustaches at a ten past ten on his face. And he must have been welcomed there with the same fanfare as before. The table must have been loaded with an equally exhaustive array of foods. Maybe pineapple pastries instead of chocolate cake this time, and rasgullas instead of gulab jamuns, a different filling for the sandwiches, but the menu of available girls must have been limited to Girl Number Two only. Would she have been instructed by her father to smile a lot or would they have manually parted her lips to see her teeth like the examination of buffaloes at a cattle fair? A toothless buffalo, her milk teeth having fallen out, would fetch a good price since it would mean that she was ready to give birth. The birth of each calf would result in two teeth sprouting in her mouth and after six teeth she was done and ready to be retired. But Girl Number Two had to show the presence of all her teeth to establish her beauty and youthfulness. The molars, the canines, embedded in the jaw in a curve well defined. Maybe her father had used that same wooden pointer to spell out the map of her teeth.

'Those people are so nice,' Balli's father said to him. 'Nobody is so nice these days, so accommodating. The minute I told them of your doubts, they were unhesitating in their invitation for us to visit again. You now have no reason not to marry her.'

'But how could you have gone there again?' said an exasperated Balli.

'You are the one who expressed doubts about her teeth, so I just went and checked up again. There is nothing wrong with her teeth.'

He would have to marry her now, not because her teeth had made the grade, but because he would have to atone for the second examination, the double display of the girl.

✳

He stared out of the window of Shangri-La and said, 'I don't really want to get married.'

'But why not?' Tejpal asked. They were at their favourite Chinese restaurant where you could order noodles and sweet-and-sour but you could also ask for dal makhni and tandoori roti, with plenty of onions. Or then you could order them all together in the true spirit of a melting pot. In the old days they would even compete on the number of rotis each could eat. Twenty, then twenty-five and onwards. It was all on the house. Balli was the established winner. Even the owner of the restaurant, Meiyang, participated in serving the competition rotis. Meiyang was Chinese, but born and brought up in Ludhiana, and would qualify as a Singh on most counts except for a missing turban. He spoke Ludhianvi Punjabi, ate kadhi chawal on Sundays as did his children, and referred to his friends as 'Bhaaji'. His relatives in Calcutta accused him of speaking Chinese with a Punjabi accent.

Meiyang, Harish, Tejpal and Balli sat around a table, going over the events of the day. Balli said, 'I don't know, but something inside me revolts at the idea.'

Unlike most people, marriage did not throw up images of hearts and roses in his mind, or for that matter access to some robust sex. Instead, it brought to the fore hazy impressions of a hospital room and a wailing baby being tossed from one bed to another, with Balli trying to grab it, saying, 'My sister, my sister.' He did not know why these shadows danced in his mind.

'Maybe we need to purge you of this brotherly sentiment that does not let you get married,' Harish suggested.

'And just how are we going to do that? Light a fire and call in the voodoo man to use his broom to exorcise the evil? Beat it out of him?' asked Tejpal.

'I was going to propose that we take him to Dhakka Colony, where all those women wearing skimpy clothes come from. Those orchestra girls who are so visible at weddings, they are all there. Let's just push him off the deep end. He will have to swim for it and we will stand by and cheer.'

'How would that help?' asked a nervous Balli.

'You are not likely to see one of those as your sister,' elaborated Harish. 'Those ones wearing little, little skirts.' Harish wriggled his posterior to indicate the littleness of the skirt, the smallness of the bottom and the suppleness of both together.

The idea met with noisy approval all around.

'Wah, wah,' said Meiyang, as though responding to an Urdu couplet. 'Bhaaji, what an idea.'

✹

Dhakka Colony was a colony by default. Like most parts of the town which had not seen anything like planned growth, it was not meant to have been there. Construction in the town was only a series of eruptions, which neither made any prior announcements nor followed any defined pattern. However, Dhakka Colony had the added misfortune of carrying a name that made its intent clear. It had pushed its way into existence but was not going to be a pushover either.

The unlit central road was a narrow alley with one-room housing on either side. The doors and windows of each of these rooms looked out on to the alley. Conversely, the occupants of these rooms provided a series of cameos to passers-by. Here was a woman in black buckling up her sandals; another one dabbing on make-up; a man emerging from his attached bathroom, wrapped in a towel with only a vest covering his torso; an oldish woman brewing a cup of tea; a little girl skipping out of the doorway. It was difficult not to see it all in one glance. There was also an urge to wait and follow the action through. To see the woman stand up in her sandals, to look at the made-up face, to watch the man pull on his trousers, to sense the comfort of hot tea coursing down the gullet as the woman sipped it. It was idle curiosity but fuelled by the manner in which these everyday people stood out in relief, in their lit up interiors, engulfed by the blackness around. And in spite of the seeming ordinariness of their lives, they became characters whose actions evoked interest, though they themselves remained oblivious to the transparency of their existence. They had a work-a-day equation with the street and therefore, did not see it as an intrusion into their lives. They neither pulled down any curtains nor kept the door shut, their quarrels and friendships unfolded under the spotlight of their sixty-watt bulbs.

There were signboards posted outside every other room. One said 'Sweet Star Musical Group' with a silver star dangling by its side, another said 'Golden Bell Orchestra', and yet another was home to the 'Melody Orchestra'. The woman who stood up in her sandals and the other who was readying her face would ultimately head out to one of the numerous weddings in town. They performed choreographed dances on stage, in groups or solo, to Hindi film songs while the wedding guests hung around and watched. They wore flashy, glittering clothes—the kind that were on display at the tailor's shop in their colony.

The tailor's shop stood at the head of the street and was the first thing that greeted you on entering Dhakka Colony. The shop did not have a name. It did not need one; it was the only one there. And it was unmistakable. Two armless mannequins stood outside. One wore a sheer black sequined skirt barely covering her plastic buttocks, and a short wrap-around choli of the same fabric on top. The second mannequin was in orange see-through, tight trousers, which too were all aglitter, with a choli to match. The tailor would haul both of them into the shop at night at closing time. He would put his arms around each one's middle and lift her just an inch above the ground. He did not want them rubbing their heels in the dust. He could not manage more than that because he was not a tall man. However, it did not involve more than a 180 degree spin around and one brief unsteady step into the shop. He would lower each mannequin on the left side of the door. Both would end up facing the back of the shop till the next morning, when they would be dusted, and their clothes straightened. Arms around the waist, the spin in reverse, one shaky step out and they would be back on their vigil, right next to the doorway. These two were the first personages that you met at Dhakka Colony, their faces smiling beatifically, their arms outstretched in a come-hither.

The flesh and blood women slept during the day and woke up late in the evening to rehearse or innovate dance steps, ready their clothes and prepare their faces for the stage. The street came alive only in the evening.

When the four friends walked down the street they felt like voyeurs caught in the act. They walked down one way and then walked back, pretending to look straight ahead most of the time though their eyeballs were dancing from side to side, catching glimpses of the women. They were not sure of their next course of action. Should they just walk up and knock on one open door or were there bouncers around who would toss them into space and send them into orbit? But if not a knock on the door then how else did one approach them? And then, what exactly were they looking for? Were they commissioning a dance performance for Balli's bedroom?

'I'll tell you what we will do.' It was Harish taking charge. 'We will walk up and down a few more times, identify the best-looking one and then approach her.'

'We should let Balli decide,' said Tejpal.

'Balli is being called upon to make far too many decisions in a single day.'

'But then it is he who has to watch the girl dance and feel something stirring.'

With uncertainties dogging each step, they made a few more trips. By this time they were beginning to get curious glances. The idlers and elders sitting on jute cots outside the rooms were following the movements of the strangers through narrowed eyes. They had once beaten the income-tax collectors out of their colony because, as they said, they were paying protection money to the don and that was as good as paying tax. Who were the taxmen to come and make demands on them? Their narrowed eyes narrowed a little more with each tentative step the quartet took.

'Who are they?' they were asking each other. 'Shall we ask them what they want?' 'Wait. Let us see what they do next.' But since the four men did not do very much other than walk up and down, a consensus started building up towards accosting them. The women were the bread-earners in this area, and the older among them began to roll up their sleeves. Even the stray dogs spread-eagled on the muddy sidewalk were now sitting up and growling under their breath. The four began to feel that they should just leave—and quickly. They would have to defer the knocking on the door to another day.

'Shall we run?' they asked each other.

None waited for the answer. They just sprinted.

✖

'Why did you have to run?' asked Harpreet later.

'Even the stray dogs were beginning to growl. I did not want them getting a taste of my ankle.'

'Stray dogs are easily shooed away. All it needs is a pretence at picking up a stone and flinging it at them.'

'Not these. They were obviously born and brought up in Dhakka Colony. They were quite at home.'

4

Sweety of the Golden Bell Orchestra had no idea that she had been the subject of much discussion among four men who had gone past her window, examining her from the corners of four pairs of eyes.

Eyeballs left as they walked from the tailor end of the street to the vegetable vendor.

Eyeballs right when they made their way back from there to the mannequins.

A vision squeezed out of squinted eyes.

Even if she had known, it would not have made much difference. She was used to being eyed by men in that certain way. However, she may have seen a novelty in the oblique angle of the quartet's stare, since the usual gaze featured moustache-twisting, naked aggression. That macho kind of gaze was a guided missile that would bore down to the very marrow of her bones. She could sense it before she saw it.

Her feet ached because of the high-heeled black sandals in which she had danced the previous night at a wedding where guests refused to let the party wind up. Considering that many of them had just come in close to midnight, carrying gifts in shimmering paper with elaborate flowery toppings and cascading ribbon ringlets, it seemed only fair that the celebration be extended till the morning, to accommodate them. And then it was only at night that a summer wedding did not reduce women to mounds of molten make-up and turn men liquid inside two-piece suits. Some of the men would even need to be carried out, though that was because of the quantities of liquor consumed.

'This summer is exceptionally hot. Oof,' the women told each other, fanning themselves, while the two-winged pedestal fan sounded like a monster that had been disturbed in its sleep.

'I don't remember it being so hot ever.'

Yet, like winter, it had always been that hot each summer. The dust chased wizened brown leaves, which in turn looked like they were going to burst into flames. Buildings trembled, refracted in the rising vapour. Colour drained from the countryside. Memories were not short. They were only erasing, abnegating, to begin again.

The men were too busy to notice the heat. They were generating some of their own.

There had been endless encores each time Sweety stepped off the stage. She had been Madhuri Dixit that night, with an intoxicated audience swaying to her movements. Drunken and delirious men with liquor glasses balanced on their heads waddled around, gyrating their forty-four-inch middles to a countdown in a film song.

Ek do teen...
Char panch chhe saat aath nau
Dus gyaran
Baran teran

One to thirteen went the numbers, as the beloved counts moments to a reunion with her lover.

'I count painstakingly, waiting for you,' sang the men to each other, and with the pronouncement of each 'you', half a dozen hands shot out, pointing to each other in drunken misdirection guided by filmed-over eyes. Others pointed her way. Glasses clinked. Some fell to the ground from the giddy heights of balding pates, where they had been placed for a display of balance. She swirled around in her black, diaphanous nylon skirt worked over with blue sequins patterned into a moon and stars.

She had been briefly upstaged when the bridal pair had made their entry. All other lights had been switched off as a pair of 2,000-watt beams shone on a wooden moon pasted over with silver paper and poised atop a sweep of silver stairs. A door had swung open in the moon, revealing its brown, wooden behind. The moon's bottom. The bride and bridegroom had appeared, then stepped through the door like visiting dignitaries alighting from an aircraft, waved to crowds below while photographers and video-wallas clicked and rolled. They walked down the stairs in a glare of flashlights and were briefly surrounded by friends and relatives, then immobilized for the rest of the evening into two high-backed, ornate chairs, which were placed on a stage that was part of the heavenly constellation. After that, everyone forgot about them and proceeded to party. The couple sat and smiled self-consciously at the video camera that was permanently pointed at them, their image projected on large screens that were placed around the venue.

Sweety was back centrestage while 'whishky'-soaked voices called out to her, 'Shhweety, you are the besht.' Some of them scrambled on to the stage, waved a wad of money over her head to ward off the evil eye and gave her the money. A man in a bowler hat had even whispered something to her about a film career as he tried to tantalize her with money that took the halo route over her head—'Come and shee me.' She had a secret pocket even in her most translucent dresses, which only hinted at anatomy without actually showing any. This was where she stashed the overflow from unbridled generosity pried loose by liquor.

The morning was different. She needed a painkiller, both for her head and her feet. Extremities were always a problem, she mused. It was difficult being astride two worlds, the fairy-tale fantasy of a wedding venue and the reality of morning. It was schizophrenic being Madhuri Dixit and Sweety. She wondered if Madhuri Dixit herself had the same problem when she did things that were routine, things that protagonists on screen never seemed to need to do. Go for a morning shit for instance. Did she fill up a mug of water to wash herself—washing the moon's bottom—and then easily reconcile this squatting image with the one on screen where she only moved in a swirl of music?

But at least she did not have to go to a bed in Dhakka Colony, and that reduced considerably the operational area for schizophrenia.

Madhuri Dixit was Madhuri Dixit for most parts of the day and night, when she reported for her shooting schedule, sparkled at an awards ceremony, twinkled before television cameras.

She did not have Kailla looking in at her window. And that was Sweety's immediate problem, other than the drum in her head that beat a steady, unerring rhythm. Who was this man, she wondered. And why was he stationed outside her window? The few strands of his beard were grass struggling to grow in the dense shade of an old tree, the folds of his turban like an uneasily balanced, lopsided rope basket about to reveal a coiled snake.

In the distance stood a group of grinning bystanders. Had she woken up as Madhuri Dixit, they would have been looking for an autograph. There would have been adulation instead of derision.

'What do you want?' she asked Kailla.

'I was sent,' said he, in the best traditions of a messenger. The carrier pigeon with a missive tied around its neck.

'By whom?'

'Somebody.'

'But who?' she said, the irritation of an aching head rising within her.

'There is a man, a big sardar.'

Kailla himself was not very clear since the instructions had come down to him third-hand.

'He might have a name,' she suggested.

'He lives in that white kothi.'

Big white mansions were many. There was nothing rare or distinctive about them. They were in Sarabha Nagar, Ranjit Nagar, Model Town. Rows upon rows of them, competing for space on the ground and in the air.

'And?'

But that was as far as Kailla knew.

✖

The four men had sat down over chicken sweet and sour, tandoori roti and a propitiating plate of noodles out of deference to Meiyang's Chinese origin, and relived their peregrinations up and down the Dhakka Colony road. Up and down went their minds, peeping in at the different windows. Too fat, too thin, either too jiggle-jiggle or a chest of drawers with two knobs. The bra size worked like the auctioneer's mallet. *Thaak*. Sold.

But on the dinner plate it did not work. What is needed is the leg and not the breast. Caterers at Punjabi weddings profess that they are on the lookout for a four-legged chicken for their business to be viable. 'Everyone wants a leg piece. Wonder why chickens could not be mammals with four legs?'

The breast piece works in bed though.

It was decided that the girl who was buckling on her sandals under the banner of the Golden Bell Orchestra was the best option. There was something erotic about a pair of black high-heeled sandals. Women in pornographic films wore black stilettos and absolutely nothing else, never worried about exposed warts or unwanted bulges for all to see. In fact, they puffed out their silicone-filled chests with a pride of possession that was very seductive. So thought all the others, though Balli was yet to discover that sentiment.

'She was nice, don't you think?' they asked.

Balli cleared his throat, his mind still full of burrs, and his heart still holding down his brotherly effusions, his knee pinning them down in a wrestling manoeuvre. He drummed a nervous tune on his knee, a morse code telling it to keep his fraternal feelings at bay.

'Don't even say that she is like your sister,' said Harish, his admonishing finger up in the air to pre-empt any such excesses.

Balli had also thought that she seemed the most attractive.

This time he was making his choice based on a squint-eyed scrutiny of her features rather than a counting rhythm. He prefaced and suffixed his expression of approval with a lot of 'umms' and 'hmms'.

'I think, though…umm…I am not sure any of this makes sense…umm…but if you insist…I think, maybe, hmmm the one that…'

It took him a long time. In the middle of it all he even shovelled in an entangled mouthful of noodles, taking extra time out to slowly and noisily siphon up a particularly long noodle that hung all the way down from the o of his mouth to his plate.

He also delivered a short, hesitant speech on marriage, which mentioned companionship and the lack of it, love and the lack of it. He spoke about the gap between love and compatibility. A gap so wide that a couple could fall through standing shoulder to shoulder. He spoke without the disadvantage of experience.

But he also expressed approval.

A cheer went up.

'Here's to the woman in black,' said Meiyang, raising the bowl of sweet and sour—capsicum, onions and chicken pieces slapping around against the dragons in the bowl.

That particular matter having been settled, there was yet the awkward business of contacting her and negotiating terms.

'You go and talk to her,' each said to the other.

'My wife will lynch me.'

'You obviously survived the last visit.'

'But that's precisely it. I can't tempt fate again and again.'

It was soon apparent that none of them would go. Dirty business. Round splatters of cowdung on the Dhakka Colony road of the same odour as the social grime attached to it. A societal pothole. Noses wrinkled in disapproval. Much easier to ask somebody else to negotiate it.

'I'll ask Kailla if he can do something about it,' said Tejpal.

'Who is Kailla?'

✖

Kailla was a pre-partition fixture in Jassi's house. He was called Shafi then. His father had worked in a hosiery unit, while his mother worked in the house. They were devout Muslims, offering evening namaaz every Friday at the Jama Masjid in Field Ganj.

Religion then, like now, like always, was a whole meal—a bit of god, a bit of socializing and a bit of politics. But for three-year-old Shafi, god was yet an abstraction, politics was only a lot of excited talk and heated speeches meant nothing. The only thing that made sense was the presence of many other children at the mosque and the games he could play with them. Yet there was some sort of charge in the air, which even the children could feel. Not all the time, but at sudden moments when an adult face went red, with bulging eyes ready to pop or an odd tremor in the voice, like the twang of a taut wire.

In the December of 1921, a rumour had gone round that Maulana Habib-ur-Rehman Ludhianvi, great-grandson of Shah Abdul Qadir who had been at the forefront of the 1857 mutiny against the British, had been put to death inside the jail. People were already in protest mode. Mahatma Gandhi had addressed a huge gathering at Daresi Ground earlier in the year exhorting the people to adopt non co-operation as a means of protest. The Daresi Ground was a circular clearing in the middle of a teeming bazaar and the entire area had once been a part of the Ludhiana Fort. It was in the Daresi Ground that the British assembled Indian troops. An English General would command his officers to give the Indian troops a dressing down—'Give them a dressing down, give them a dressing down,' he said, and the ground came to be known as Daresi Ground.

In 1921, crowds had poured into the Daresi Ground to listen to Gandhiji, and as revolutionary words like non-cooperation and satyagraha filled the public address system, the assembly stirred to the call for change. Thereafter, the people fine-tuned satyagraha into strategic action in accordance with the resources available to them. At the end of that year, a hundred blind students from the madrassa raised slogans in front of the clock tower, led by their teacher, Muhammad Yasin. Then the Muslim, Hindu and Sikh women marched in the streets to protest the killing of Maulana Habib-ur-Rehman Ludhianvi. The police had to bring the maulana out of jail and show him to the public. But a handcuffed maulana was even more incitement to join Gandhi's satyagraha. The Muslims of Ludhiana stayed firmly with the Indian National Congress even when there were calls from other parts of the country demanding Pakistan.

Perhaps that is how Shafi had chosen to stay on in this sprawling house when Partition finally took place.

He was a jaunty young man working in the same factory as his father, where he learnt the art of weaving fabric on a loom, which became his specialization. As part of his duties for the day, he was also required to escort Jassi's sister-in-law, the daughter of the house, to college and back. He would carry her books and follow her faithfully, perhaps half in love with the idea of being in love, imagining for himself the role of a persecuted lover who dared to fall in love with a young girl from a rich family; his fancy fed by the many love legends of Punjab—Heer Ranjha, Sassi Punnu, Sohni Mahiwal, Mirza Sahiban.

He would usually be slaying monsters as he followed his charge, clearing his beloved's way of any dangers that beset her path. A swipe from Vincent A. Smith's *Oxford History of India* would catch the monster square in the middle of his forehead and it would collapse in a heap. His beloved walking in front of him would be oblivious to the flurry of events behind her.

When she got married and left the house, Shafi had mooned around for a bit because that was a requirement of the role he had assigned to himself. In the main house, when they noticed, they thought he was missing her just the way a brother should. But by then he was playing the role of a jilted lover and the agony of separation had turned into indignation.

Therefore, it was not for the maudlin demands of love that he did not leave when the nations got divided. It was for the drama in his head. Monsters climbed out of it and walked up the Ferozpur road to Bharat Nagar Chowk and on to the Mall Road where he slayed them. He addressed phantom gatherings at the Daresi Ground while on his way to the Ludhiana Fort where the British had set up a textile-weaving unit and a massive boiler with 'John Thompsons, Wolverhamptom 1924' written boldly across it. The fabric that came off the looms was also called 'Ludhiana', shirting material which was a muted, almost mousy mix of white with very dark grey, and which formed most of Shafi's inexpensive wardrobe. He would be cutting across Daresi

Ground whistling a tune of his own making, when the vast expanse of the ground would suddenly draw his attention and the temptation would be too strong. He would succumb.

The blink of an eye would raise a rostrum and he would be standing next to the Gandhi and Nehru that he pulled out of his head. He stretched out his arms to the people in appeal, then raised a finger to make a point—'Khaddar, wear only khaddar. None of this foreign-made mill cloth'. 'Shafi amar rahe, long live Shafi!' he heard in his head. There would be wild cheering. He would make an even greater impact than the national leaders. Next day, all of Ludhiana would be talking about this rising star on the political horizon, or so he imagined. The flesh and blood Shafi would make his way to the textile unit only as Shafi the weaver, the rhetoric of his long speeches sitting like coiled recording tape in his head, ready to be rolled out when it was time for play.

His mind was the landscape of the city. It swirled outwards from Chaura Bazaar and made its way down all the narrow lanes. He was in his late twenties when the rest of his family left for Pakistan, though his spirit was still skipping down the exciting pathways of his teens. In any case, he had not thought that the choice was so final, that the divide would be so absolute that he would be parted from his family forever. Later, news floated back that everyone had been massacred, apart from an uncle and a cousin.

He had to hide in the house like a fugitive, licking the wounds of his sorrow, till the killing of Muslims abated. For a while his mind was a snowy screen where there were no images. He would climb the fruit trees and sit on one of the branches, hiding amidst the leaves, his chappal-encased feet occasionally giving him away, as he swung his legs to his own rhythm. The household absorbed his withdrawal with a quiet patience. But gradually, the mischief in him resurfaced and he would fling the missile of an unripe fruit to announce his presence when he spotted someone in the backyard. When things stabilized, he resumed going to the Jama Masjid, except that the masjid was now a gurdwara. Shafi, having grown up exposed to both religions, made his peace with this new Jama Masjid where he did not offer namaaz but listened to kirtan instead. He grew his beard, rubbing camel piss and onion juice into his cheeks to get a more luxurious crop. He did not want to be a khoda sardar, a turbaned Sikh without a beard, the object of social ridicule. He then wrapped a cloth round his head in the semblance of a turban, and from Shafi he became Karnail Singh. The name was a derivative from the army rank of a colonel and the most appropriate choice for Shafi, who was a belligerent guardian of the house.

The day he made the formal transformation he travelled to Anandpur Sahib, the hub of Sikhism. Wearing the five accoutrements, each beginning with the letter 'k' and therefore referred to as 'kakaar', he appeared before the priests. He was checked for his steel bangle (the kara), for his uncut hair (kesh), the little comb that held the knot of hair in place (the kanga), the sword (the kirpan), that was slung on his side, and at last the long underpants (kachera) that he wore under pyjamas, which lay folded at his feet as he faced the inspection team.

He wondered if the women, who waited their turn behind the men, would also be asked to strip to their underpants to prove their allegiance. In that case it might have been a better idea to have let the ladies go first. But as it turned out, the women were taken into the fold fully attired and on the assumption of compliance on the length of underwear.

The bhai, as part of his priestly duties, examined each of the men like a nun in a convent school checking for bloomers under skirts and for clean fingernails. It took a whole sweaty day and was enough to discourage the weak-hearted from any pretensions to Sikhism. Karnail Singh was then administered the sweetened water which signified his official entry into the Sikh fold. Since there were no rough edges to his adaptability, Shafi had fused into Karnail Singh much before the clamour of this ceremony. And even though the Jama Masjid once again became a mosque in 1956 at the insistence of the prime minister, Pandit Jawahar Lal Nehru, Shafi continued to be Karnail Singh.

And from there on to Kailla was easy.

By the time that Jassi came into the house after her marriage, Karnail Singh was already Kailla. When a stroke left Jassi's husband paralysed, Kailla gave up his job at the textile mill and for four years bathed and changed him, massaged his legs and arms with warm oil, and carried him to the toilet and then the open veranda every morning and evening. But the evening entertainment was Kailla's specialty. That was when he was at his creative best, uninhibited by convention, innovating as he went. He would pull on Jassi's cast-off petticoat and kameez to perform a mujra—swinging his hips provocatively, rolling his eyes seductively and celebrating the ridiculous with complete abandon, while a tape recorder belted out sexy film numbers.

Jassi's son and daughter also grew up on a Kailla diet.

'I can make people disappear. I can turn a man into a broomstick, a jhadu, and stand him in a corner of the room,' he would tell them. 'That is what I do when big people misbehave.'

The children were sceptical. 'How can you do that? You are not a magician.'

'Remember when I went away last year for six months? I had gone to a magician and lived with him and learnt his magic.'

Kailla had indeed gone away for six months but it was only to learn swordplay from the martial nihangs. In those days he wore the designated blue robes and a two-feet-tall turban, which hid many talismans in its folds and which was so heavy that his neck sometimes tilted over like a stem loaded with a double dahlia.

'Then do some magic for us,' the children would plead.

'No, no. It is not a game. I perform magic only when the occasion demands it.'

The children would once again challenge him. 'You are saying this because you can't change anyone into a broomstick.'

'Why would I lie to you? Come, I will show you.'

And he would lead them to the kitchen.

'Do you see all those huge kundi sottas on that shelf?' he would say, pointing to the black stoneware mortars and pestles that are part of every Punjabi kitchen.

'They were all men once but now they have turned into stone because they were wicked.'

The black mortars and pestles, against the backdrop of a white wall, may have looked innocent in the day but in the dark they were just shapes. Admittedly not human, but they were nevertheless poised for action, as the pestle stood upright in its base. They were personages with potential.

Kailla had a story for each of these.

'This one you see, this pestle. It is smooth at the top. Feel it. This used to be a bald man.' The pestle was worn silky smooth, having been worked for years grinding rice for phirni, wheat for angoori barfi, lentils for making the batter for bhallas.

The children, more exposed to turbaned heads than bald heads, felt it and marvelled at it.

'Was he really? And what did he do to become a kundi sotta in the corner of the kitchen?'

'He ate children. He is, actually used to be, the King of Sunet. You know the one that I told you about.'

'The one who lived on that mound near Ludhiana and ate human beings and burped loudly? Then the old woman whose child he swallowed cursed him and upturned his kingdom into the mud like it was a bowl of porridge?' The horrible bowl of porridge, the dalia they had to eat every morning, was the easiest thing to upturn without any qualms, thought the children.

That was the thing. Bad deeds brought cataclysmic results. Rubbed the nose of civilizations into dust. Actions did have their consequences.

'What did the bald man do this time?' asked the children.

'He continued to eat human beings. So I had to turn him into a kundi sotta.'

That then was Kailla justice.

'Should I turn him into a sotta?' Kailla had thought when his uncle from Pakistan came to visit him many years later and had boasted about how he had avenged himself by killing many Hindus and Sikhs on the other side of the border in that bloody August of '47. Kailla had happily forgotten him as soon as he left and had gone back to teaching the children a song.

Come children, let me give you a window to Hindustan,
Mark your foreheads with the mud of this land,
This is the land of sacrifice.

And the song went on to list the heroes of India's struggle for independence from the British. However, in Ludhiana the history of Indian Independence was rapidly becoming the history of its industries. Stories of the meteoric rise of big industrial houses were becoming folk legend. The heroes were those who chartered planes, holidayed abroad, weighed down their women with jewellery. The trouble with this galaxy of heroes was that they were not from the past and were therefore subject to the vagaries of time, and so on occasion, one would fall through, bankrupt.

In the bazaar, shopkeepers were slowly hammering down the thick walls of the Ludhiana Fort to increase the sizes of their shops. They had to wet the walls and keep them soaked to soften them for slaughter. The walls would not give way otherwise. These were no ordinary walls but had once been the stronghold of the mutineers of 1857 when they seized the Ludhiana Fort. But now the remnants of its ramparts stood like the one odd tooth in an old mouth.

'No veer rasa, no juicy heroism,' Jassi would tell her children.

Over the years, the children grew up and went away to other lands; the elders, their grandparents and father died, leaving behind Jassi in the house and Kailla in the outhouse.

The textile unit where Kailla worked also changed character. When he had worked there in his teens, the weavers usually broke up for namaaz. Then came a time, after Partition, when the unit was starved for workers and Kailla had become a master craftsman at the knitting machine. Of late however, there was a new influx of workers, who were coming in by the trainloads from Bihar and Uttar Pradesh. There was a 'kisan special' that came from Benaras to the Ludhiana railway station twice a week and each time disgorged hundreds of labourers. In the seventies they had come in response to a changed cropping pattern in the fields of Punjab, where there was a seasonal need for extra hands. They came and they went. But now they were manning the power looms and lathes in the Ludhiana industries. They stayed in their own colonies, the cloth shops selling saris, the sweetmeat shops selling gujiya, the general merchant selling 'chokra sabun' and 'sri gange tel', a rail reservation agency catering to the home visit once a year. This was the Hindi heartland in Punjab.

Kailla was a frequent visitor because his friends at work lived in Indira Colony. He would also periodically fall in love with one woman or another in this locality, fascinated by the rings in her feet, believing that he was still young enough to get married.

So Kailla acquired yet another layer to his persona, of the Bihari from Bihar. He took to speaking a mix of Punjabi and Hindi and added Chhat puja to his list of propitious days to be celebrated. He would join the kilometres long procession that slowly made its way over the Phillaur Bridge with the river Sutlej flowing below. Vendors would sprout up alongside—balloons and baubles, chaat and channe bhature, tea and pakore—as the devotees made their way to pay obeisance to the setting sun; then again in the morning to catch the rising sun, setting afloat lighted earthen lamps on the water body. The town would turn up its nose in disdain at this collective visibility of an alien culture. Travel advisories would suggest that motorists should not attempt this stretch.

Kailla would be there in the middle of it all, carrying a basket-load of raw coconuts, sugarcane, home-made puris and earthen lamps on his head. Born a Muslim, practising Sikhism and now a Bihari among 50,000 Biharis. These were not layers that were a protective covering for the kernel. They could not be peeled off to reveal an entirely different Kailla—one that had been well hidden, one who had to offer namaaz. The layers themselves were the essence. The layers were Kailla. Like an onion, each peel was part of the whole, each were integrally the same.

✖

Today, Kailla had walked down the Dhakka Colony road, past the puncture repair shop—'Pancher fix', past the meat shop—'taaza murge ka meet', also translated into 'frash cock meet', and stopped at Rajhans Studio—'photografs in 20 mint for Rs 20 only'. Life-size cutouts of Madhuri Dixit and Sridevi, even if a trifle stunted, their necks deep inside their shoulders, stood just inside the entrance. He stuck his right arm around one and smiled down at the woman in his embrace. She is smiling in the other direction, he thought. He moved to her right, his left arm around her. She smiled up at him.

An amused audience gathered outside the shop, entertained by the incongruity between an old man and his teenage sentiment. Some looked, laughed and went away. The idlers stayed on, waiting to see this through.

Nobody thought of getting me married, thought Kailla. His resentment against fate was only a mule track in the landscape of his mind. He had strayed onto it just now because the cutout had smiled at someone else even as his arm encircled her. That was the thing about fate. It always smiled at others and reminded him that he might have been married but for the workings of chance. It reminded him to grumble. He murmured to himself.

'Want a photograph?' Ramesh asked, peering through his lens, his left eye tightly shut, double images edging their way into unison. He had a winner there. His cutouts were inspired by the tailor's mannequins, which, he had noticed, seduced even the most casual passers-by. After an analysis of its benefits, the idea was executed in cardboard and topped with faces of film stars powdered over with dust from the road. It worked. He had only recently put his tentative toe into business, swirling it around to test the waters from scalding hot to comfortably cosy. Only two years ago the Khalistanis would have shut his shop, might even have killed him in a fervour of propriety. In those days it was best to minimize your visibility and seem as though you were not there even when you were. Those men with long, flowing beards would not have approved of this new hussy face, one that compelled a gaze.

Kailla hesitated. Became coy. But then, had his picture taken in a sudden rush of brazenness.

'Chadi jawani budde noo,' said one of the idlers derisively. An old man trying to be young.

'And why not?' said the youngster who wore a visor backwards. 'Look at all those oldies running our country. You have to be eighty plus for life to begin.'

They all grinned broadly, their teeth gleaming in the sunlight.

'Keep at it, keep at it, lage raho,' they advised Kailla.

They were waiting outside for him when he emerged from

the shop, and followed him to his next destination. They had nothing else to do.

They were part of the background when Kailla approached Sweety's window. They watched the mute show from a distance, scripting dialogue, providing their own soundtrack for the exchange, betting on possibilities and guffawing loudly with a distinct desire to give offence.

5

Gurjant Singh was a dud firecracker, sputtering in situ, never really blazing into the sky. He was a leftover of the insurgency, a bad aftertaste. He survived when others died at the hands of the police. He had remained on the fringes then, when all the others, similarly wired, had been wielding AK-47s. He only liked the posturing that it allowed him. He liked the aspen fear that it evoked. He liked the sense of commitment he could subscribe to without having to make a heavy investment. It only involved growing an untamed beard and configuring a fierce face.

When all his armed comrades were talking the language of the gun, he was getting into wordy disputes. At one such incident he had sprung out of his chair in the very last row during a seminar on Punjabi poetry and objected to the speaker referring to Guru Nanak as a poet.

'He was our Guru, the founder of Sikhism and a saint. Not a poet. If you make this mistake again,' he told the speaker, 'you will be eliminated.' The term resonated with memories of lucid letters, hand delivered, signed by 'generals' of the Khalistan Liberation Force, Khalistan Commando Force, Babbar Khalsa International, threatening dire consequences if...

Gurjant strode up to the mike, past the seminarians, whose arms burst into pimpled gooseflesh. He stood towering over the dark little woman with short black hair who had made the blasphemous statement and already felt a little ridiculous for having used a hammer to swat a fly. It spurred him on to greater heights of threatening rhetoric.

'Our panth, our religion is not to be tampered with. When we form our own nation, people like you will be done away with at once. At once!' he shouted, his voice cracking up, raggedly torn asunder into different decibels and tonalities to let through the force of his emotions.

'It is not an insult to be called a poet. That too is an exalted calling, consciousness at its most evolved, capturing the silences that lie between words,' said the little lady looking up at him from somewhere in the region of his belt, holding to the square inch of ground under her feet and using seminar language as though responding to an issue that had been thrown open to the house.

'Actually, both poets and saints usually sit on the fringes of society,' she added as an afterthought. 'It is only the offal of religion that tries to push centre stage,' she said, hinting at Gurjant's grabbing of the mike and his ungainly thrust into the limelight.

'A poet is of this world. But a saint is different,' he shouted. He too felt those intervening spaces that she talked about, though his were filled with grime. But he did not have the pretty words needed to contend with the little lady. His sensibilities needed a mysterious god up there, even if it took a certain amount of shuffling around of gods and saints to install one. He did not want God becoming the next-door neighbour. He repeated himself, 'A saint, not a poet'—in that same loud voice of a defeated argument.

The firmament is Thy salver
The sun and moon Thy lamps;
The galaxy of stars as pearls strewn.
A mountain of sandal is Thy joss-stick
Breezes that blow Thy fan;
All the woods and vegetation
All flowers that bloom
Take their colours from Thy light.

—The little lady recited Guru Nanak's verse and asked, 'Is this poetry or is it not? Devotional poetry, but poetry all the same.'

'If he was a poet and only human,' said Gurjant, thumping the speaker's rostrum, 'then how come he performed all those miracles, wringing water out of stone, getting Mecca to move around?'

She was not to be moved.

'But the gurus were at great pains to emphasize their humanity, not their other-worldliness. These saakhis are to be understood as metaphors. When it says that he moved Mecca around it was only to point out that God is everywhere, not just in temples, mosques and gurdwaras.'

'You are trying to downsize our religion.'

'But I too am a Sikh.'

'Then why are you wearing your hair short?' His pitch was still at rafter level and he no longer knew how to bring it down without losing face.

But the more he ranted, the more did the difference in their heights stand out in relief—and the more foolish he felt. The audience was transfixed. At other times they would have sniggered, but not now. Would he pull out an AK-47 and spray the assembly with bullets? They waited, minimizing themselves in their chairs. Is this how they would die? Seated in their chairs, at the verge of making a point and then going up in a cloud of pointlessness? Should they crawl under the hoof-shaped seminar table? But that might only mean precipitation. They waited for Gurjant to pull out his gun.

Suddenly, he stormed out like an angry husband crossed in argument. Just like that. He was followed by his assorted collection of hangers-on who tried to wither the gathering with their looks as they swept out in a burst of indignation. The last of them turned around to deliver a final, over-the-shoulder killer glance, like a ramp model just before disappearing between the curtains.

Gurjant and his team had been similarly belligerent when an Odissi-dancing husband-wife duo had performed an oeuvre piece, choreographed to the strains of a shabad. They had prepared this one especially for their Punjab visit, selecting the hymn with care to evoke a propitious opening, the man had said.

The man's bare upper torso glistened with sweat and necklaces, his red-spangled lungi sparkled under the stage lights. He did not know that he was severely underdressed for this particular undertaking. Heads had to be covered for the rendering of a shabad, combined with a stillness of stance. And here is this shamelessly naked head threatening to dance to a shabad, thought Gurjant.

And that too in a state of undress.

And definitely no dancing.

And not with that hairless chest.

His sense of manhood was clearly defiled by the sight before him. A man had to walk as if he had a lemon wedged under each of his armpits. Of course, that is not how he put it to himself since he took a much more serious view of the entire business of being a man. But since messing around with the attributes of manhood only took him into dark depths— some known, some unknown—he leveraged his faith instead, putting it into gear for confrontation.

He is even wearing necklaces and rings.

Kohl in his eyes!

Bloody homosexual!

It made his stomach turn to see a man, a topless one at that, dancing in this effeminate way. A topless woman he would go with, but this was gross. Sisterfucker, thought Gurjant.

He and his non-playing team stormed into the wings, even as the dancer was reciting the verses to which he would perform.

From the perspective of the audience, the dancer's subsequent behaviour remained inexplicable. Every twenty words he looked into the wings, then every ten. Five. Two. One. His head was on a spring, bobbing up and down and left and right. Finally his gaze was completely swallowed up by the curtains. A half-sentence ricocheted in the hall, looking to complete itself. But, for the dancer, his audience had ceased to exist. He himself became the audience, transfixed by that which only he could see.

Gurjant was performing what appeared to be a war dance, in the wings. He was gesticulating madly to convey his affront. His actions mimed a neat slicing of the throat, a display of bare nipples as he twisted two points on his shirt front into little knobs, and the firing of a gun. The dancer got the message and hurriedly walked into the wings, his ghungroos setting up an agitated tinkling as he went.

The performance was cancelled in the interest of all concerned and Gurjant had achieved this with his bare hands, without AK-47s. But that was then.

Now that wearing a gun was no longer fashionable, put out of vogue by the police crackdown, Gurjant had taken to carrying one. A countrymade pistol, the kind that would explode in the hand of the shooter. Or it could be jammed and create a comic villain who clicks and clicks and clicks, but never fires.

He had threatened Sweety with it, exhorting her to stop dancing on stage.

Sweety had thought, in a perverse sort of way, that this might be a good way to die, alive one second and dead the next. No death throes. You could die laughing.

'If you do have to kill me, then you might as well put aside that gun of yours and plant a bomb on me instead,' she told Gurjant.

His gun was not loaded. That was his sinister secret. Not even his hangers-on knew this. His countrymade weapon was only a cosmetic intervention, false boobies deployed in the industry of sex. His entire existence centred on a display of bravado. His dream was to watch the world quake as he strode past it, to see all of humanity tremble before him, to see people on jelly legs letting down a quiet trickle of fear.

'Don't give me smart answers,' he said, shaking the pistol in her face, starting up a delicate breeze with it.

'Why don't you do something else for a living?' she asked him.

'That is my business,' he said righteously.

'Then how come everybody else's business is your business?'

Sweety was being facetious, and Gurjant did not like

it. Threats had to be taken seriously in order to be threats, otherwise they were not worth the breath expended on them. And he was beginning to suspect that he and his pistol were not having the desired effect. In fact, he had the distinct impression that they were working like a feather duster, gently tickling the senses. Sweety looked like she was about to smile, but it was quickly siphoned up by her eyes, before it could burst at her lips. He would have to do something more severe to evoke gravity.

That was the trouble with these guns.

His own had always been undersized. When he was little and a keen participant in the 'shoot a piss' competitions, his pee would invariably rain down on his own toes. And, since then, there had been a steady lack of adequate growth.

One could grow out of the habit of eating candies and into the mature desire to eat the much-despised vegetables of the gourd family; one could grow into the desire to go early to bed; one could just simply grow fat or thin, as the case may be, each in opposition to the intended end.

But in Gurjant's case it had been that he had not grown at all in that one area of concern. Rather, so little, as to be seen as not having grown at all. He could now aim past his toes and just clear the inner rim of the piss pot.

He had even gone to one of those men who offer miracle cures. The ones that offer to increase a penis to the size of an elephant trunk; promising the sexual prowess of an acrobat.

The hakim, his head crowned with a tall turban, sat on the floor in a colourful, makeshift tent which had the dimensions of a little room. Nath Baba claimed that he was from Himachal Pradesh, and it was from the mountains that he brought all the herbs that went into the making of his medicines.

'From far up in the mountains,' he said. 'Sometimes you have to stay in the forest the whole night and wait for the first rays of the sun to fall on this medicinal plant, through the early morning dew, before you pluck a few leaves. It is not easy.' These were no dime-a-dozen popping-pills that pharmaceuticals churned out in industrial quantities, which one could buy off anonymous shelves in chemist shops. They were custom-made. The hakim not only knew just when to pick the first leaf warmed by the first rays of the rising sun, but also knew the problem that you were coming to him for.

'A small one? Yes?' said the hakim.

And Gurjant was completely overawed.

Gurjant had hoped that the cure lay in that line-up of jars that stood poised for a group photograph—little ones in front on the ground, taller ones on a shelf that ran right around the tent and still taller ones on pedestals at the back. Little globules like pinheads, bigger ones like ball bearings, still bigger ones like table tennis balls, floating in brine or rose water or sitting cheek to cheek in jars.

'Yes, small,' said Gurjant, losing some of his inhibition, since the secret was already out. 'Sex is a problem.'

'I know. I could see it on your forehead when you came in.'

What did his forehead have to do with the size of his penis, he wondered. Was the smallness of his member advertised on his forehead and had he been walking around all over town like an open book? Did people laugh behind his back when he had gone by? Did they jerk their thumbs his way and say 'did you see that'?

The hakim gave him ten little packets with ten little globules in each of them. He had asked him all kinds of questions. Do you shout when you get angry or do you only grumble under your breath? Do you go for a shit as soon as you get up or does it come only later and what colour and consistency is it? Do your palms itch? He had then meditated for a while to arrive at the right globules. Gurjant had fidgeted with his hands, his buttons, his watch, his turban, his moustache, all the while that he waited. Finally he was told that he was to swallow the contents of one packet of the pinhead variety, each day, on an empty stomach, before he went at the fried paranthas. On the eleventh day he would be a new man, with a brand new penis. After the visit, he would carefully open one packet every morning and funnel the globules into his mouth. When the occasional one got away, hiding amidst the sheets or bouncing its way under the bed, he would be down on his knees, groping, then coming up for air and a torch, since it was pitch dark under the bed; and then he would dive under once again. He could not afford to lose that tiny but potent bead. It might well be the source of that extra micro millimetre.

However, he woke up as Gurjant Singh of the little wee wee even on the twelfth day. That made it all the more necessary for his countrymade one to find veneration. He, Gurjant Singh of the 'short'-gun fame, needed to take a more perilous route to recognition.

6

The road to Mr Bakshi's house was winding strangely. The last they knew, and that was not many days ago, just six as a matter of fact, it had kept along the Sirhind Canal and was straight as an arrow. But here it was, meandering so, almost like a mountain road to an inaccessible peak.

'Keep to the centre of the road,' Tejpal told Balli.

Balli was driving with the vigour of a truck driver, swinging the wheel, his hands flying over it as he alternated his grip to take the turn, first left and then right. His wheels would kiss the edge and Tejpal would shout, 'Watch out, watch out!' Balli's hands would go into a desperate retrieval dance, as though shaping ladoos in the air, forming perfect globes out of sweetened dough.

'This sisterfucker road,' he said.

But as it turned out, the road was quite as straight as ever, it was just that Tejpal and Balli were negotiating it through brains that were swimming in scotch whisky.

Balli had insisted on driving. 'Of course I will drive. Why, why can't I drive? I am perfectly in my senses. You think I am drunk?' he had asked, taking great umbrage at Tejpal's hesitation to ride with him. 'I am not drunk. Don't think

I am drunk,' he had said, the alcohol sloshing from side to side in his cranium.

'No, no. You are my brother. I will go anywhere with you,' said Tejpal, hidden tears in his eyes and voice, his loves and hates greatly sharpened in his mind over the last few hours with the repeated clinking of glasses. They had had to do the last few cheers very studiedly and carefully though, since they were beginning to miss each other's glasses. He had been everywhere with Balli. He had gone to Dhakka Colony with him and now he was sitting in a car that was only inches away from diving into the Sirhind Canal or flying off the embankment into the entangled undergrowth. This, most certainly, was anywhere or nowhere.

The wheels of the car once again negotiated the tightrope between life and death. In this state of mind it was not possible to distinguish one from the other, to tell between the hullabaloo of life and the hoo-ha of death, or between a man and a bush, a tree and a truck. The road too kept appearing and disappearing like an illusion. The twilight made it worse. Danger was no longer danger but exhilaration. It only strengthened the belief in the drunken lore that an invisible cushion lay under one's butt in case of a fall.

Believers presume that god, or those of his ilk, have a special love for drunkards. This lore grew and prospered because those who had driven off the embankment had not lived to tell the tale. And those who survived were that much more convinced of the existence of that eight-inch foam which miraculously appeared under their falling form, unrolled straight from the heavens.

Balli and Tejpal made it though, without any emergency celestial intervention. Past the lone, lost cow. Past the man on a cycle. Past the truck loaded with ugly aluminium chairs that boasted red velvet upholstery for a large wedding somewhere in the vicinity—a man sitting atop those chairs, ready to unload them when they reached the venue. They could see the glow from the wedding lights burning into the sky. When they arrived at Mr Bakshi's gate a party was in progress. They swept into the driveway as though on the trajectory of a mountain bend and on that same elevation of spirit.

They had started drinking early in the evening, much before the sunset hour. It had all started with the arrival of a government notice that threatened to take over Balli's father's land for the development of an industrial estate. In Ludhiana the industrialists were envious of the tax exemptions that the agriculturists were given and agriculturists, in turn, felt that they were being circumscribed by land ceilings whilst the industrialists expanded unchecked. The two, farmer and factory owner, were always threatening to edge each other off the earth. As Tejpal's father had told him, there is only so much land on the planet. Only that much space for everyone to exist. Back then he would not have known about land reclamation though, about boulders being dropped into the sea to create land and landing strips, about man playing god. About god abdicating, trounced out perhaps, by man's upward aspirations.

Initially, Balli had laughed about it, saying, 'Good enough. Ultimately we can all eat cycle parts instead of wheat…. or then, penis,' he said as he spotted Jeeta, the old family retainer, coming in to serve a bowl of peanuts. Jeeta never got 'peanuts' right, though he could have just called them by their Punjabi name—'moongphali'. But Jeeta wanted to be able to throw in that odd English word. And so he offered 'penis' to Balli's guests. While the men guffawed, the women burned with embarrassment.

Balli's father had, in fact, attempted to set up an industry for cycle parts in the fifties because he was convinced that ultimately, the man at the driving wheel would be the businessman.

He had named his outfit Zygon Industries. The name had come from his desire to be contrary. Most people wanted names that began with an 'A', because that ensures first place in a line. The line at the estate office, at the registrar's office, at the magistrate's office. However, the line was only in the head, if at all, since most places that required a queue usually degenerated into a moving mass of jostling elbows, a press of bodies and eyes peering over shoulders. No one stood in a line anywhere. But Balli's father had thought of going to the tail end. 'Z,' he had thought. And then, since he was already at that end of the alphabet, he had tried both 'X' and 'Y' to go with 'Z'. But the former offered only impossible tongue twisters, zxytic, zxotic, zxmon… He had finally arrived at Zygon.

It was a false start. He had no idea of how to keep track of the nuts and bolts that keep the axles in place. He had piled them high like stacks of wheat in the single room. There were no inventories. The workers went home with pockets full of nuts and bolts. They sauntered in when the morning was well on its way. No one knew how many axles should be produced in the course of a day to ensure a profit above expenses. The production rate was whimsical.

The factory had to be shut down while others went on to become cycle tycoons. Thus Balli's father had gone back to growing wheat with the resignation of a martyr and an air of superiority about the wholesomeness of his occupation compared to the stinking sleaze of business.

In any case, agriculture was looking up just then, looking up to the US from where a Ford Foundation team had arrived on invitation from the Indian government to study ways of increasing wheat production. Ludhiana was chosen as the prime location for their pilot project. They were introducing Mexican seed, which was slated to give three times more yield than the local stock.

Balli's father had been fascinated. These Americans come equipped with everything, he had thought. Years later they even went to war outfitted with television and chewing gum and popcorn, where they sat in their tanks, watched television and ate popcorn, apart from going out there to kill and be killed.

When they arrived in Ludhiana they had their beer bottles. Budweiser. The American researchers and farmers had lunch together everyday. A working lunch. And out came the beer. Jeeta, a lot younger then, would carry Balli's father's lunch to him on site. In those hot summer days, when the sun would burn holes in their heads, lassi would be the essential starter to lunch. His wife would send a huge thermos full of buttermilk for him.

'What is this you drink every day?' the Americans asked Balli's father.

'Lassi,' he said, but then realized that the word meant nothing to them. It did not conjure up images of languid summer afternoons, of cooling down as lassi coursed down the gullet, of headiness induced by two big glasses of lassi, a healthy drunkenness summoned out of the good things of life with no moral laxity involved, of the long siesta that was a must. He knew he had to explain. As the shortest explanation of all these delicious images in his head, he said, 'Indian beer.'

'Oh, we would like to try some,' said the Americans.

After all, they were exchanging technologies. They might as well exchange beers too. There was a ceremonial give and take of glasses. The Americans loved this 'Indian beer' and wondered why it was not marketed and why they could not buy it off the shelf. From that day onwards, they drank lassi and Balli's father drank Budweiser. The arrangement met with the satisfaction of both parties. It was only when the Americans asked for Indian beer at a party that the truth of it all emerged. They had refused to talk to Balli's father after that.

But his acres began to prosper by the seventies. His house on the farm had been a courtyard surrounded by an unbroken row of rooms with two fans ineffectively whirring away the heat as best they could. The toilet on the roof had been a bricked-in chamber pot. When the Mexican seeds became wheat in the market, every room had its own fan and plumbers were called in to install pipes and drains and flushing systems. Every room now had its own bathroom. These attached bathrooms were a measure of the good things of life. His farmhouse had become a palace from where a car carried his only child to school everyday.

His prosperity did not produce more heirs for him, though. Strangely enough, his wife's second pregnancy a few years later ran its full term but produced nothing by the end but a lot of hot air, gossip about how it had only been a tumour, or an illegitimate child, or a pillow tied around the stomach. Why would nine months of carrying around a distended stomach produce nothing, not even a stillborn child?

So Balli was the only son of a prosperous landlord, and was to inherit all those rich acres. But now he was angry that the government might inherit it instead.

That is why he had swung into the driveway of Mr Bakshi's house, though of course Mr Bakshi had nothing to do with the threat of it being taken away. Mr Bakshi was only tying up with some foreign buyers for the supply of still more pullovers and mufflers. He had no idea of the resentment with which two individuals were riding to his house.

Balli and Tejpal stepped out of the car and were immediately swallowed up by the swirling party. But not for long.

Initially they had mingled with the guests and made not-so-polite conversation since they were on a wavelength that lifted them above the usual niceties of life. But soon enough the issues about land were rising up from their stomachs like an ill-digested meal, threatening to discharge a burp with an offensive odour.

They had gatecrashed, but Sarika was gracious nevertheless, insisting that they stay for dinner. Balli bowed low over her hand, almost kissing it, though that would be a gesture entirely alien to his Punjabi sensibility. Guests were beginning to look his way from the corners of their eyes. There were suppressed sniggers. A drunk offers juicy dramatic potential.

'I would love to spend the night with you,' he said, 'but I have to go.' Loosely interpreted into more acceptable sentiment, he only meant that he would have loved to stay for dinner but was hampered by his own liquid state.

Just then he spotted Mr Bakshi.

'You, you,' said Balli, his finger pointedly sticking under Mr Bakshi's nose, 'you stop swallowing up our land. You are not satisfied with what you have. You want to eat up everyone's share. You leave my land alone or I will shake the teeth out of your head.'

'You farmers are a pampered lot. No taxes to pay and yet

you go around with an injured air as though someone has robbed you of your rights.'

'You know how hard my father had to work. And things were never available. He had to go all the way to Ferozpur to procure one can of diesel for the tubewell, tractor and thresher; plead for electricity, plead for water. You people keep a generator right in the middle of a locality, have thick red wires running into the house and start making something and money. An ice factory maybe. Dirty ice that makes people sick.'

'And what about the wheat you grow? What you finally sell has generous quantities of mud. Just listen to the rubbish he talks. I have seen him this high,' Mr Bakshi said, indicating the region of his knee. 'I have even seen him naked.' An indrawn breath from the goggle-eyed gathering, particularly the foreign buyers, who immediately jumped to the only conclusion that such a statement warranted, which was slightly misplaced since all Mr Bakshi meant was that he had seen Balli as a toddler, when nakedness is not shamefulness.

'Are you saying we purposely dirty our own wheat?' An angry Balli was incredulous.

In 1885, the Deputy Commissioner of Ludhiana had conducted an inquiry and found that wheat was mixed with mud pellets and that there was a ready supply of these available in different sizes and colours to suit different kinds of grain. It was the traders, not the farmers, who made the blend. A hundred years later they were still talking about dirty wheat.

The argument got louder, uglier and more irrational with every exchange. The only sensible way of settling such arguments was a decisive punch to the jaw.

'You!' said Balli angrily.

But, like always, Balli's finger pointed in the wrong

direction, because Mr Bakshi was completely innocent of the alleged crime. Balli had then stepped forward to dislodge Mr Bakshi's teeth. The assembled company hurriedly stepped in to rescue his teeth from harm.

Balli and Tejpal were soon regurgitated from the party. Unceremoniously. And they once again sat in the car for a hair-raising ride back home. Balli's confidence was undiminished. Tejpal's faith in Balli's driving skills was a little rattled but propped up by the sentimentality of a childhood friendship.

7

'It's all these guns. Turns their heads,' Jassi said.

Harpeet had been talking about her husband's snoring. She usually became quite animated when she talked about it. It had such dramatic narrative potential. Much more exciting than just a story between book covers where one's imagination has to lift events out of the pages. She alternated the 'khrrrrrrs' and 'pheeeees' with the practised ease of a virtuoso.

She talked about how his cover sheet rose and fell, pitched on a stormy sea. Of the brief moment of silence when she would check to see if he was still breathing, and would then retreat startled, when he would roar back into the next round aloft a hungry lion. Of the whistles and trebles that emanated from him in slumber.

She had no idea how guns suddenly became a part of this exchange. But then Jassi had become hard of hearing of late and the conversation usually skidded along a giddy path, slipping into side lanes via homophones. Had she, Harpreet, said something about 'runs' or was it 'suns' or for that matter 'sons'? Any of those could have triggered the deviation. Especially sons.

They ended up discussing sons and the great Indian love for them.

Jagga jamia te milan vadhaiyan,
kevada ho ke daku ho gaya.

When Jagga was born there was much merriment,
And when he grew up he became a bandit.

This was Jassi's favourite ditty. And even though legendary, Jagga's banditry was not genuine villainy but revolutionary zeal, quantified into a large swathe of sand, nine maunds to be precise, getting soaked with his blood after he was shot dead by the British. Jassi still saw him as the boy who deflated the dreams of his parents.

'All this fuss about having a son and then when they grow up they are drilling holes in their parents' heads,' she said. 'Now look at that Inder. What she did makes my stomach turn even now.'

'Inder who?'

'Your friend Balli's mother.'

'Balli's mother?' said Harpreet, stupidly echoing Jassi.

'You seem to have caught the deafness from me,' Jassi said, her years giving her immunity against the social codes of pleasantry. 'Yes, Balli's mother. Two daughters were born to her after Balli. But where are they now?'

Harpreet had no idea of course. She did not know that they had ever been born and therefore was hardly likely to know of their present whereabouts. However, Jassi clarified things for her—one had disappeared from her crib in the hospital soon after she was born, while the other had died under very suspicious circumstances.

Harpreet heard the tale with growing horror.

The doctor at the nursing home where the first baby disappeared had told the story with great pride. 'Right here in our hospital,' he used to say, as though he had done the baby a good turn.

There were two beds laid out side by side in a private room. Two women lay there wailing. One because she had had a miscarriage and the other because she had given birth to a daughter. Both thought it was the end of the world. Both thought that fate had dealt them a tough blow and were shedding enormous tears, which were swamping their cheeks like a river in spate. But grief has a way of building walls around people, sealing them in high towers, making them feel exclusive—so that the women felt that their respective sorrows were far more potent than anything that had happened before. It was, therefore, after a while that each of them registered the caterwauling of the other. They removed their wet veils from their eyes and exchanged notes.

'But why do you want a girl?' said the one who had just given birth to one, amazed at the quaintness of the other's need.

They came to an arrangement.

The woman who had lost her baby would adopt from the one who did not want the baby. The dead baby would be Balli's mother's instead, to wail over and cremate. And that would set the record straight. The hospital and the doctors concerned looked the other way while an informal adoption took place. Little Balli watched his baby sister going away with the aunty in the next bed.

Harpreet said, 'Oh!' and suddenly understood Balli's vision of a world inhabited by sisters.

'Duniya rang rangili,' said Jassi. It takes all sorts to make the world.

They had reached that stretch of their morning walk along the rail line where it was necessary to hold a hanky to one's nose and wear blinkers over one's eyes. This was the slum settlement where parties of children organized themselves every afternoon to conduct raids on Kailla's fruit trees. In these early hours, the railway track acquired a scalloped edge from the many bottoms that sat there for a morning shit, facing the train, which was only a passing audience. Here one minute, gone the next. There was no shame in being seen by those who would quickly melt into the mass of undifferentiated humanity. The anonymity of their bottoms turned towards the settlement, they figured, would save face for day-to-day living.

It was this stretch that deterred Harish's wife, Sarika, from visiting Harpreet. The rest she did not mind, she said.

'You have such a simple lifestyle. It is so sweet,' she had said simperingly, clearly not meaning a word of it, and taking in the two rooms in a single glance. 'How do you manage, though,' she had said, in an inadvertent slip, which she quickly covered up with effusive praise for the three-legged stool, the four-legged dining table and the five-cornered makeshift kitchen.

'How different.'

But the smell en route she could not take.

Somebody with an irregular constitution had chosen to perform his morning ablutions at the exact moment when she was passing by.

'Why on earth don't they go do this somewhere else? No shame, really. Sitting there in full public view. I tell you we Indians have just no civic sense.'

'Actually they are from the labour colony across and I don't think they have much choice,' Harpreet had said.

Did she think they had an attached bathroom but preferred to offload under the sky just as they exercised their freedom to fart in public? If you keep it bottled up inside then you are likely to rocket forth into the sky at some point of time in your life—this was the subject of many Punjabi jokes in which Santa Singh finds himself deposited in Japan straight from a Punjabi village as a consequence of having expended wind. As children, a fart always occasioned considerable giggling as they lay under their mosquito nets beneath the sky and heard their grandfather's uninhibited fart. He would be half asleep, ensconced in his own mosquito net, many beds away in the line-up which followed the family hierarchy, the eldest first and down to the youngsters who made up the far end. They could even imagine him lifting one side as he let fly, and they would usually dissolve into helpless giggles and smother them in their pillows. They need not have bothered though, since this was a moment of such singular concentration and catharsis for their grandfather that he would hardly have noticed even if they had been rolling over with laughter. They might however, be admonished by their respective mothers, though in a conspiratorial, 'we understand' sort of way.

But exigencies in life always blurred the lines between private and public life. And the exigency of the lack of a private toilet was bound to take the shame out of a shit.

'No, no, these people just don't want to better themselves,' said Sarika.

'I wonder why,' Harpreet said sarcastically.

'They just don't have the sense. You remember Sarla? The sweepress? She is going to have another baby. Soon they will have taken over the earth and people like you and me will be looking around for some obscure corner.'

She then pulled out a bottle of perfume from her designer handbag and gave herself a generous spray even as she mouthed a disgusted, aspirated 'ouf'.

She had never come over after that.

The smell was quite offensive though, even if Sarika's reaction could be dismissed as the squeamishness of the rich about all things that smell less than Chanel. But both Harpreet and Jassi had learnt, this being their daily route for a morning walk, to inhale deeply just before, as though readying themselves for a stretch underwater. They did not want to change their route. At least here they knew exactly when they should inhale and when it was safe to breathe again. Smells could not make a surprise sally into their nostrils.

So all conversation ceased just then. That was the nice thing about these companionable conversations.

Having negotiated the smelly stretch, Jassi took a deep breath, more from the fact of having held it for so long than as an accompaniment to the sentiment she was going to express, and said, 'Boys are callous, girls are such a comfort.'

Her son had given her no reason to arrive at this particular conclusion. He was a doctor abroad and was as attentive to her needs as a twenty-hour flight with two stopovers would allow. Her daughter was her favourite though.

As they walked, the aroma of ripening mangoes filled the air. For everything that goes wrong there is always something that goes right, thought Harpreet. For every lungful of faecal breath there is the heady fragrance of chausa mangoes.

If you were not in films and only living life, then things fell back into the commonplace of ups and downs, the rhythmic see-saw of festivities and mournings, quite quickly.

Jassi did not agree though. She had seen enough drama in her life, she said, to have developed a chronic sense of anxiety. When her husband had developed high sugar she had dreamt that he was pissing sugar cubes. When she told the doctor of her dreams, he had only been pragmatic. 'What is there to do? Just gather up the sugar cubes and you have your month's supply.'

As a young girl she had packed her small tin trunk and come to the Indian side of the border when the country was partitioned. 'If you can carry a spoon instead of a ladle, do that,' her grandfather had said when she was leaving, as a sort of larger statement on travelling light, and from the certainty of coming back once things had settled down. It had rained incessantly that August of 1947.

They had spent the following winter as refugees, wrapped in cotton veils because their woollens lay layered with neem leaves in large trunks back home. Her brother, with a chapati in hand, had asked her mother, 'Beeji, have we become beggars?' They hadn't really, but they had pretty much scraped the bottom of the barrel.

Rain is something of a mood enhancer, thought Jassi, as she recalled that August drenched in blood and water. If you are happy you dance in it, if you are sad you cry with it. But when clouds do gather in the sky and the rain comes down all of a sudden on a nondescript day, there is panic, the danger of getting wet far outweighing the danger of being run over on the road—two wheelers will drive blindly, pedestrians will dash through the rain blind to the oncoming speeding car.

'In our time even the weather was much better behaved,' said Jassi, obliquely referring to the wayward ways of the young. 'It played no tricks. My mother used to tell me that when the British were here fifteenth of September was the official onset of winter. The manual operator of the fan would be put on another job.'

'He must have lost his job when electricity was introduced.'

'Maybe he was then employed to remove and put away the wooden wings of the fans and wrap the remaining stumps on the ceiling in cloth. And then on October fifteenth the angeethis would be lit up by him because that is when winter began according to official orders.'

The cycle of seasons too obeyed these official orders.

But in this August of '95, forty-eight years later, the monsoon had failed. An occasional shower, only good for dirtying feet and paws and for generating unsavoury smells. Wet pet paws on drawing room floors, mud-caked shoes drying in verandas. Not good for much else. Certainly not good enough for the crop in the fields.

'Too damn hot,' said Harpreet, grumbling and wiping the sweat from her brow. 'I could just melt away and would have to be collected in a bucket.'

'My grandchildren, when they visit in summer, think that I have turned on the heating. "Switch it off, nani," they tell me. I tell them of the man up there in the sky who has all the controls. And they wonder why they can't see him and appeal to him. "Who is this guy?" they ask me.'

Her grandchildren, in keeping with the expatriate spirit, struggled to keep up with the loaded business of being both American and Indian, of being able to say 'sat sri akal' and 'hey dude' in the same breath, of sporting underturbans as a mandatory part of their religion and yet regarding their headdress as the American freedom to be different. They had learnt the names of the ten Sikh gurus but if, when reeling off their names, they stumbled, then one would ask the other, 'Hey, what is the name of the eighth guy?'

Harpreet shared a name with Jassi's grandson. He too was called Harpreet. Sikhism was gender equal when it came to names. Other things being unequal, as in most other religions, societies, worlds.

Harpreet had been named even as her mother braided her hair into pigtails for her first day at school. Until then she had only been Baby, the youngest child in a household of many. Her eldest brother was Harpreet Singh. Running out of ideas and time, her mother had said, 'Shall we call you Harpreet too, Harpreet Kaur?'

She was quite happy to be Harpreet.

Playing hopscotch with their own thoughts, the two of them, Jassi and Harpreet, had reached the head of their lane when they noticed a figure standing at their gate.

'Can that be…?' asked Harpreet.

Jassi was equally incredulous.

'Your eyes are young; you tell me,' she said.

'It is,' said Harpreet.

Sarika had come, wading through the smells and slush.

'Papa has disappeared,' she announced, when they reached her.

Mr Bakshi had indeed disappeared. Her father-in-law had worn his favourite white shoes that morning. This pair was as white as his shiny white teeth. His shoes were a measure of his mood. He wore them when he was feeling on top of the world. In spirit they were his high boots, the kind that the hunter wears when he stands beside his trophy, one foot atop his kill, to be photographed in all his glory. But now he had disappeared, white shoes and all.

8

Mr Bakshi's white shoes were sitting on the floor next to the bed, one shoe lying across the other, like a fork and knife crossed in a plate signalling a desire for more food. The superstition was that one shoe riding another was a sign of impending travel. In the case of Mr Bakshi, however, the journey had already been made, quite against his will. He crossed his arm over his eyes and wished that he did not have to see the ceiling, where a crack in the whitewash wended its way right across and suggested a possibility of the roof caving in. What you could not see did not hurt, even if you were only pretending not to see it—a tactic that was part of his survival kit. Mahatma Gandhi had also told the nation, through the example of the three monkeys, not to see, hear or speak any evil, though his exhortation was more an injunction to steer clear of evil rather than as a means of self-deception. For Mr Bakshi, this instinct came from the hand his mother extended over his eyes to prevent him from seeing things she did not want him to see. 'No, no, don't look. This is so horrible. Look at all that blood. Terrible accident. Hai rabba…' And though he could not see the bloodied man as he lay there choking and gasping, she would feed the picture into his imagination. Which is why he now occasionally peeped at the ceiling from under the crook of his arm to make sure that it was holding out—seeing and yet not seeing.

The fan whirred reluctantly, hanging by a claw from that same cracked ceiling, groaning with the effort, hammering out an unvarying rhythm—khat khat khat khat khat, and kht kht kht, discarding its vowels when the electricity voltage increased. Hmmm hmmmm hmmmm went the mosquito in tandem. It sang persistently in his ear. He tried to swat it away, clapping his hands over it half-heartedly, but missed it altogether and watched it float with graceful ease up to the ceiling. The sound of the clap had startled the silence, like a gunshot in the night, and he thought he had best let the mosquito be. Would it survive if the roof fell through, he wondered. It was an idle thought, but then he did not have much else to do. Idle thoughts were all that were available to him and he was willing to pursue them so long as the burden of consequences fell on the mosquito. He did not want to speculate about his own fate because that would mean dwelling on the bloated form of the body that would be found floating down the Sirhind Canal. Some would say it was the police that had put it there to cover up its policy of elimination without trial, while others would say terrorists had got tired of lugging him around, from hideout to hideout, and dumped him there to get rid of excess baggage. If his kidnappers wanted to swap him for some money—a few lakhs maybe—then there was still some hope. He had no idea what he was up against or what he was worth.

One minute he had been strolling in his driveway, wearing his elevating white shoes, ready to leave for work, working up an appetite for breakfast and feeling an intense sense of well-being while his thumb lovingly caressed the amount on the cheque in his hand. The next moment he had become a portable bundle, parcelled into a blanket, stamped, labelled and posted to an unknown destination, journeying in a car boot on a potholed road. All this was conjecture on his part though, since he had no idea what was happening to him or where he was. The darkness was absolute. It was the kind of darkness that surrounds you when you wake up and grope around for the light switch, then find it is no longer where it used to be, and then realize that you are on an unfamiliar bed. It was a strange, unyielding darkness, viscous with fear. This is it, he thought. When the blanket was thrown over him at the moment of his abduction, he had quickly balled up and swallowed, after assiduous chewing, a cheque worth ten lakh, though his insides retched at the strangeness. His eyelids had automatically closed tight with the weight of the blanket. His eyeballs, pressured down with an unrelenting hand, had square stars dancing in them, little geometric shapes that appeared and disappeared, then winked their way to an exit and floated in yet again. He had been lifted off his feet, like a child, while his white shoes kicked the air.

As a child his mother had wrapped him in her veil and hoisted him on her shoulder to carry him across the newly defined borders between nations. Someone had lifted him and deposited him in a truck. Even as he had been dumped into that truck he had felt like a piece of cargo. He had clutched his mother's veil tightly around him and concentrated on its nearness. All the while that they had journeyed through seething fires and spilt blood, he had been tracing, with his finger, the diagonal lines of the lehriya on the veil that covered his face and form. The parallel lines ran down the length and journeyed to the edges of the fabric. He had stayed the course of those lines with single-minded devotion.

But travelling in the boot of a car was new and intimidating. The reassuring diagonal lines were missing. It hurt to be pushed up against hard surfaces, to feel the sharp edges of apathy, of unbending metal. His flesh endured the impact of the potholed road. His senses touched the blackness, longing for familiarity, but finding only a malevolent strangeness.

In the boot of the car, he thought he must no longer be alive. He lay there, a foetus in embryonic darkness, but without the promise of birth. He must be dead. And if he was not, there must have been some mistake somewhere. When they finally lifted him out of the boot, he realized that he was not dead, as he had imagined. I'm alive, he thought with a measure of disbelief. The bruises hurt and assured him that he was indeed alive. He felt no exhilaration at the discovery, because what do you do with an existence that is smothered in a suffocating blanket in the middle of summer, with sweat trickling down from the nape of the neck, along the spine and into clinging underpants, where it spread into a dampness onto the seat of the trousers? He was only a body that was being tossed around like a sack of potatoes, lifeless and unresisting. The kidnappers had then deposited him into yet another vehicle, but this time he was sitting on a seat, registering sounds of undirected traffic that lurched and swerved, screeched and honked, and missed you by the width of a whistle's breath. Were they driving through Chaura Bazaar, where vehicles treaded on each other's toes in an ungainly dance? It was not a spacious bazaar, as the name suggested, and there was hardly any room for negotiating a vehicle through the chaos that prevailed. It took nerves of steel and a persistent hand on the horn to carve out a path through it all.

All the while he was thinking about just how 'strugglesome' his life had been. This was a word he used often; its existence in the English lexicon was not of deep interest to him—in fact, he was singularly confident of its evocative powers to describe his travails through penury on to prosperity. Because, as he often said, 'I have got flow of English and good knowledge of English.' And that precluded any attempt at correction to a standard which had been set by someone else, somewhere else, and which did not recognize his personal equation with English. When he was spoken to in Punjabi, he responded in English with a generous sprinkling of 'sirs' and 'madams' in an effort to display his breeding. His use of articles and prepositions was peculiarly effusive. 'Myself the Mr Bakshi,' he would say, whilst introducing himself.

He hoped this was not his whole life flashing before his eyes in a sudden premonition of death. He had heard stories of how his grandfather knew that he was dying and how, days before his death, he had begun talking about his past, had begun to see his elders standing beside his bed and beckoning to him, while those attending to him had become invisible. They had been at pains to tell him that he was only seeing things and that it was a delirium of fever and that he should in fact, be acknowledging the reality of those around him. But he had gone quite firmly into flashback mode and announced to the world at large that he did not have very much more to do with this life; it was time for him to go.

✸

Mr Bakshi was deposited on a bed in the room with the

cracked ceiling, after a long journey. The room was spartan enough to be the setting for a hermit's sanctum sanctorum. In a corner sat an armchair with one arm missing and a table with joints that quivered to the touch. The blanket that had, till recently, covered him and under which he must have passed out before he was deposited here, was carelessly thrown over the one-armed chair. Only the nail hammered into the door contested for attention with the crack in the ceiling, a riveting presence in the isolation of his incarceration.

He wondered what his family would be doing back home. His son and daughter-in-law must be asleep yet, working off the excesses of the party they were at the night before. They clocked a different sunrise from the one that was stated in the newspaper every morning. For them, the day began when they woke up. Even my children have not appreciated all my efforts, he said to himself. What is it to them? They got all this readymade. He was thinking of the wealth that made it possible for his wife to order around the many servants to ready his breakfast. The smell of paranthas being fried with oodles of rarified butter must be filling the air. His nostrils inflated as he inhaled deeply on that delicious aroma. But it only made him aware of the gaping hole in his stomach. Would they, the kidnappers, merely starve him to death? No loaded gun. No pressing down on his oesophagus with the power of a well-applied thumb. Just plain starvation.

'You are going through a bad patch, these are bad times for you,' the pandit had told Mr Bakshi. 'You must take half a kilo of black lentils, one kilo of wheat and a handful of rice every Tuesday and immerse the whole lot in running water if you want to ward off the evil that is now hovering over you, as indicated by your stars.' He was supposed to have followed this regimen for the next twelve Tuesdays. He wished that he had paid heed to this advice. After all, he had consulted this same astrologer when his son was to have been born. His wife went through a caesarean operation to make sure that their son was born at the right time, under the right stars. He had been meaning to get started from the coming Tuesday. The delay had only been the result of something as innocuous as the location. Should he go to the Budha Nala, which was a minor tributary of the River Sutlej and might therefore qualify as running water in the astrologer's book of abracadabra? However, in reality the Budha Nala, once a perennial stream of clear water, was now nothing but stagnant water and grime, layered over with pollutants from the factories and waste from the city. While the river gathered history on its shores, the Budha Nala gathered effluents. There he would have to hold his nose and discharge his celestial duties. He could also go to the Sidhwan Canal, a seasonal irrigation canal, which bifurcated the town and was the hotspot for all such immersions, though he would be at risk of breaking the law under open skies. The city administration had imposed Section 144, prohibiting easy movement in the area, precisely for all those unhappy worthies who had been to a pandit and were looking for heaven-born solutions. He could join the rows of early morning visitors to the canal, as they stood clutching their lentil-filled polythene bags, prepared to make a hammer throw as far into the waters as possible. Yet another option was to drive to the river, half an hour away from the city.

He had not gone and now he could not go.

He had tried the door with its wart-like nail to attempt an escape. He had pulled with all his strength. He had placed his foot, shod in its white shoe, against the wall, to give himself some leverage, and then he had heaved and tugged and cajoled and sweated and abused. The door had been immovable, obdurate. He had stopped a while to catch his breath. Then he had gone at it again. 'You motherfucker,' he told the door, not conversationally but with strong overtones of a challenge. 'You think you are smarter than me? Try this for size!' and he had kicked it with his white shoe. He was not, of course, offering his shoe to the door but was saying this only to emphasize the enormity of his kick. The door had been unmoved by the intensity of his frustration. Its nail-wart did not even quiver, and it had continued to look back at him poker-faced. No creak, no groan. He had made as if to kick again but then changed his mind because that pair of white shoes was a particular favourite. He did not want the point of its toe to cave in. He had waited to see if his exertions had been noticed by those who had brought him here, and who would certainly not look kindly on any attempt at escape. There was no sound. He had stared resentfully at the door for a few more moments and then gone to lie down on the bed, defeated. When he had removed his shoes they fell in a cross on the floor.

9

The police came to pick up Kailla, saying everything added up except perhaps his age, but they would have to overlook that for now since times were bad, and things suspicious were things suspicious, irrespective of mitigating factors. He was anywhere between sixty and eighty and hardly likely to be running around toting a gun and pressing it to weak vertebrae. He had looked the same ever since anyone could remember— eternally old or eternally young, depending upon where his years were pegged. He could be anything from a teenager to a prematurely greying middle-aged man, to an old man who had preserved himself well.But then he was also a Mussalman, dressed as a Sikh, behaving like a Bihari. It was difficult to reconcile all of these and still not notice any jagged edges that should have been there. They felt around for these, in anticipation of tripping him up on the facts of his ethnicity.

They asked him why he had stayed back and not gone to Pakistan with the rest of his family during Partition. He did not tell them about the giants that he had killed as he followed his charge to college, about the heroism in his head. Had he visited Pakistan? No? He must have, they said. No, he said yet again, bewildered by their insistence. You're lying, said one of the men in uniform, poking him in the ribs with his rifle. Did anyone visit you from Pakistan? Aha, your uncle? Your uncle indeed! They all say that... Uncles on hire, as many as you like. Did you go to one of those terrorist training camps they run there?

He had no idea what they were talking about and, therefore, an emphatic no seemed the right answer. Then you do know about them? He had to say no once again. They did not believe him. If you know that you have not been to one, then you do know that they exist and what they are. We will find out, they said. And then you have had it.

They asked him why he had become a Sikh. He had no answer. He had just become one. All he had to do was grow a beard, which was in any case an in-house affair, a simple matter of farming in one's own backyard. No land deeds, no title disputes, no labour problems. He had not shaved for a few days and the beard had followed its own growth logic, with very little help from him. They had not bought into the naiveté of his responses.

You went to Dhakka Colony the other day, did you not? You even had yourself photographed? Yes, he said, but he had not known that it was forbidden. How did they know that he had gone there, he wondered. The long arm of the law, or was it a giant eye in the sky? They had shoved him around a little as a foretaste of things to come. Don't you play the fool with us, they warned, pushing him in the direction of their parked vehicle.

It was a still day, so still that it did not even seem to be breathing, lest it reveal itself and be called upon to bear witness to the sequence of events. The scorched leaves were waiting for the rain to wash them down. Everything was taut with the tension of heat and suspended dust. Kailla stood with his sweaty shirt clinging to his back, and the dusty haze of the atmosphere reflected in his clouded, uncomprehending face.

They had wanted to know Kailla's date of birth. He had never felt the lack of knowing one so far. It had seemed fine enough to have been born. He had never gone to school where they might have asked him to write down his name, father's name, date of birth, religion and much else, squeezed into dotted lines too few to accommodate all this information.

'Happy Birthday to you' sung in an enthusiastic tunelessness and celebrated with candles and cake had not yet become fashionable, so there was no occasion for Kailla to notice that he did not have a 'happy birthday' date.

He had not needed a ration card because his name was added on to the family's card where he was listed as a domestic help, and that had ensured the half kilogram of sugar allotted to him during the days of rationing.

He had never wanted to vote either, not because he had any strong opinions on the matter but because the choices between contesting candidates seemed identical, where Sant Singh and Natha Singh were one and the same thing. He was not counted in the census when it happened every decade. He would usually go up into his trees when officials came round to note down the names and dates of birth of all the inmates in every household.

His date of birth was a matter of pure speculation, a derivative from many other things entirely unconnected with the matter at hand. His grandmother used to say that when Shireen, his cousin, started to make pigtails, he, called Shafi then, was only a baby, and she, Shireen, must have begun making pigtails when she was ten years old. And since Shireen was born about ten years before Mahatma Gandhi addressed the nation from Daresi Ground in Ludhiana, Shafi, being about seven years younger to her, must have been about three years old then. An assorted collection of disparate facts like these were strung together to form a sequence, much to the smiling satisfaction of all his relatives.

The month was a relatively simple matter. 'It was very cold when you were born,' she would tell him and the tone of her voice implied that it was somehow his fault. 'I had to carry buckets of hot water in for your mother.' Being his mother's son, he had obviously inherited her culpability. 'It must have been the month of Poh, or maybe Magh.' The year and the month, Poh being mid December to mid January in the Indian calendar, were trouble enough to calculate, so she never got round to pinning down a date on him. He could have chosen anything, from the first of the month to the Indian Republic Day on 26th January, anything from Poh to Magh. He had mulled the dates over in his head but had never fixed on any one because he had never felt the need to.

The absence of a date of birth in fact, was really a stroke of luck. It engendered in him an unshaken faith in the perpetuity of his youth. It gave him a certain free play with time. If Jassi occasionally, affectionately, admonished him, 'Kailla, you must act your age,' noticing that he was talking incessantly of some woman with toe rings on her feet, Kailla would look entirely unabashed. 'You should have found a girl for me and got me married,' he would say. 'It is still not too late. And in any case, what is my age?' he would add, more as a rhetorical question.

But just now it seemed very important to have a birth date to get these 'policias' off his back.

'Twenty-sixth January,' he said in a sudden moment of decisiveness.

It did not go down very well with the men in uniform.

'You are trying to pull our leg?' said the rib-poking policeman. 'You think we should be toasting you as a national hero just because you have given us this fanciful date of birth? Even Mahatma Gandhi was not born on that date, though he is the father of the nation.'

Kailla had obviously made the wrong choice in this moment of crisis. Would it have helped if he had said fifteenth instead of twenty-sixth? But now, it was not possible to take his words back.

The neighbours were out in their front verandas and gardens, trying to see and yet not be seen, to mingle with their surroundings, white kurta pyjamas merging with the whitewashed walls, eyes looking through the green hedge.

Jassi had heard the commotion and come out to see what was going on, although she expected to find only the usual— stolen fruit, fleeing children and Kailla in hot chase. But she spotted a load of policemen instead.

She tried to intervene. 'But what has he done?'

'That, we will find out,' they told her.

'I can vouch for him. He is a very good man, there must be some misunderstanding. He is really not the kind to mess with the law.'

'These are cordon and search operations, and we are instructed to carry them out with a thoroughness that cannot be compromised,' said one of the policemen.

'He has been lurking around in strange places,' said another. 'Places he should not have gone to. Times are bad and it is our job to examine anyone or anything that looks suspicious.'

One of them probed the nearest bush with the end of his rifle. The bush revealed a startled bird, which instantly flew away, resulting in a slightly awkward moment of embarrassed authority, which was quickly covered up by more bluster.

'Come on, you. Don't waste our time. We have not got all day.'

They were not going to take any chances with this bird in hand.

The 'bad times' referred to were, like the joker in the pack, useful to whip out when all else failed. 'Bad times' was the logo that had so far emblazoned all their transactions, personal or public, even though these bad times were gradually becoming a thing of the past.

They marched him to their blue matador, five policemen on either side with their weapons poised, anticipating an assault from some unknown quarters.

'In you go,' said the policeman, as though offering Kailla a secret door into a magical world, an exclusive entry into a club reserved for the elite. But he was only being pushed into the secured vehicle, the iron bars like a neatly woven handloom across the window. The doors were shut behind him.

He stared out at the checkered scene with a resignation that was not new to him. He had learnt, early on in life, to accept things as they came to him and make what he could of them, even if they appeared in the form of handloom squares. Kailla was not fighting the world. He was just living it differently.

There were more iron bars at the police station. These were not checkered but in even stripes like the pyjama from a night suit. But he could only feel them, since it was pitch dark, the day having gone by in extensive questions and answers.

When he had tried to grope around for the switch that would turn on the light, a voice had said, 'What is it? You can't rest in peace?'

He had instantly stopped, startled into momentary submission.

'What have you done?' the voice asked.

'Nothing,' said Kailla.

'You spend a night here and if you haven't done something so far, you will,' was the ominous reply.

'Will they kill me?' Kailla asked.

'You just stick to the rules and you will be all right,' continued the voice.

'What rules?'

There was no answer from the voice in the void.

Kailla had no idea what rules it was talking about. As far as he could see, or not see, in these circumstances, there were no rules of any kind. It seemed more like a free for all.

He found a wall, leaned against it, and slithered all the way down to the floor, waiting for morning to come.

10

When Kailla disappeared, the Bring Balli Back from the Brink of Bachelorhood Campaign came to a grinding halt. Balli had not been very cooperative to begin with, straining at the bit like a shy bride, both willing and reluctant, his ambiguity resulting in a gruff, disinterested manner, a 'hmmf' that was both consideration and disapproval. He had imposed so many conditions that it became impossible to locate the right place, to identify the right time and to create the right ambience for Sweety's performance.

'Not in my house. Not in yours either,' he had said.

'Try the moon, in that case,' his friends told him helpfully, taking their cue from old romantic songs that featured the moon when it was still a part of lovelore.

Kailla was to have been the ombudsman between the dancing girl and Balli, but after the police picked him up, the momentum was lost in a number of other pressing preoccupations. Finally, Balli's mother, Inder, the one who had traded her baby, was taken ill. So ill that Balli was completely diverted into the tasks of fetching and carrying blood and urine samples, collecting laboratory reports, consulting doctors, buying medicines and injections, and worrying till his head hurt. There was nothing ostensibly wrong with her, yet she was bedridden. Her already ghostly presence began to recede still further into oblivion. However, long-forgotten memories still asserted themselves, making her eyes appear as though they were trying to turn inwards, to spin around in their sockets and spot something infinitesimal, which she was straining to see. Her skin was like thin parchment stretched across her bones, so taut that a mosquito could break a tooth on it in an attempt to bite.

They took her into one of those hospitals that looked like a hotel, with potted plants and a café in the lounge, uniformed men and women as nurses, front office personnel, patient care specialists, public relations wizards, all of whom said 'please' and 'thank you' with unfailing regularity and a generous smile. Piped music, however, was of the religious kind, kirtans and bhajans, which gave the game away. This was no hotel but a place where disease and misery had a front office, where a smiling mask hid the dying throes of the patient and the devastation of those left behind.

It was at this smiling front office that they entered details of her age and the history of her afflictions, though they could only talk about the palpable ones—diabetes, blood pressure, arthritis. Balli's finger moved down the printed list in the form handed to him across the check-in counter. He ticked off her ailments, though none of those explained why she was their ghost-in-residence, flitting about the house with purposelessness; or why it was that she only came alive when it was cleaning time and she became a fiend with a broomstick and dusters; or why her hands were always moving to defend herself from something, which only she saw and the others did not; or why she said things which no one understood.

Initially they had rushed her to the Intensive Care Unit where the cardio monitor sounded like an electronic bird, an egret—ti ti ti teen, ti ti ti teen—persistent and unvarying, its monotone becoming a throb in his head. 'Ti ti ti teen,' sang the electronic egret in his head. It continued to sing for long afterwards.

His mother stabilized and was moved to a private room. She lay imprisoned in a bed with railings, and a nurse came in breezily at five every morning and suggested a bath, slapping down a fresh set of hospital attire on the bed. Even if there was nothing much that medicine could do, at least she could provide her patient with a bath. So thought the nurse, and in any case that was part of her job profile, so the sooner she got started and finished, the better for her. She could then sit down to a satisfying cup of morning tea. Balli's father would cheerily visit her later in the day, rubbing his hands with a gleeful air as though events had taken a most gratifying turn.

'So, how are you this morning? Had some breakfast?'

He was not of course, looking for an answer. They had lived their lives with words that only echoed back to each of them, cleanly bouncing off the other. When she told him of her headaches and backaches, he was not listening. When he told her of how the secretary of agriculture in the government had quaked before him, she had heard not a word, his vainglory entirely wasted. The hospital had only solidified this insularity into visiting hours, binding it down to that one hour in the morning and occasionally for one hour in the evening.

She has really become an old hag, thought Balli's father, his own youth being that magical secret between him and his mistress in Manali, which became a glow in his deepest being. He had to rub his hands now and again to release some of the charge which this glow had generated in him.

Secrets, like food, have good calories and bad calories, ones that add to the fat and others that work it off. However, the health quotient of secrets cannot be measured in terms of their acceptability, or the lack of it, by a stiffly moral society. In fact, the more unacceptable the secret, the greater its power to give off a radiance; the more secret the secret, the more its voltage. Balli's father's cheeks, though his beard hid them from view, flushed a sunset red each timehe thought of his mistress in Manali. His secret was doing him a lot of good.

Inder's was doing her none. It was, in fact, singularly responsible for her general decline.

Outside her room, they were washing down the hospital corridors, sloshing water all around and then drying it up with long-handled mops. This cleaning up, thought Balli's father, as he opened the door to make his way back, Inder seems to have brought it with her here too. Do they all have their instructions from her? I am obviously in the way.

Then he gingerly stepped over and dodged water puddles and swishing mops and was gone.

But he would have to be back sooner than he had thought, and much sooner than his mandatory morning visit when he would be bursting with its thoughtless bonhomie.

Inside the bathroom, Inder let the attendant scrub her back. She was too weak to protest about undressing before a stranger, too weak to mention that she found the water very cold on her back even though it was only September and real winter would only be here by November, or that her fingertips became like raisins in the cold water, dehydrated and wrinkled. In any case, she did not want to acknowledge the coldness of the water because it dredged up even more memories best kept dormant. The attendant was thorough, whipping up a lather that stood up in peaks like beaten egg white. Each new peak increased her sense of satisfaction and made her think of it as a job well done. The egg white then washed off on to the floor in a great mass of resistant foam, which gathered on the drain cover, waited a while there and then sank through, making gurgling sounds like a happy baby.

'You have only one child?' said the attendant, who had been watching the comings and goings of father and son.

The conversation never got any further than that because Inder, in response, fixed her with a baleful look and the breakfast trolley soon came rattling down the corridor. Ghosts did not eat breakfast but Inder got hers in a tray that sidled up to her on silent wheels astride her bed. Cornflakes and milk, egg and toast, butter and jam. She could not eat anything.

'I cannot eat,' she said, in a laboured whisper.

'Try a little,' said the attendant, coaxing. 'Your son will be here soon and he will want to know what you have eaten.'

Balli walked across the squeaky clean hospital floor and tried to introduce a spring to his walk in an attempt to lift his sagging spirits. His shoes squeaked each time he lifted his foot. It was embarrassing to be walking down the length in that hush-hush atmosphere, drawing attention to one's state of well-being. The floor that he was walking on had perhaps been paid for by Mr Bakshi, or at the minimum, its upkeep came from his pocket.

✴

Mr Bakshi had made a generous donation to this hospital because it had earned him an income tax reprieve, and also because an act of philanthropy looked good, not only to the world at large but also to himself. He had got up from his chair after signing the cheque because he thought he heard applause. The mirror on the wall opposite, which offered a clear line of sight when he stood up, was the added incentive. He surreptitiously stole a glance at himself. Apart from the reprieve in income tax, donations could also earn a reprieve in heaven, an assured place for him amidst rivers of milk and honey. But according to the Hindu way of thought, there are no rivers of milk and honey in heaven. In fact, there is no heaven at all since souls are legging it from one birth to another, exhausting the 84,00,000 lives—all of which are a necessary part of progression, like a trainee who has to work his way from the front office to the top slot by going through the grind. The ultimate destination is only a state of beinglessness, a release from the cycle of birth and death. It is Islam that offers a honeyed heaven. Many centuries of coexistence had resulted in an osmosis of cultures, such that Mr Bakshi was not even aware that he was borrowing a vision.

This particular hospital had Hindu antecedents which meant that his money was in the right hands. The other, the Christian hospital, was all right if you only needed medical cure; but for the soul you had to come back to your familiar gods and goddesses. The Christians could make their peace by donating to a saint-something-or-the-other hospital. Not that he had any great animus against the Christians since there were so few of them around anyway. But his father had had a horror of Christians. When somebody had suggested that he send his son to a missionary school, he had reacted like an overheated engine, sputtering and hissing, 'My son is no Kristaan, wagging tail of the Angrez.' That is how they were seen in his day as they went about spreading English education and denouncing some of the existing Punjabi social practices. Even though the only missionary school in town was the most sought after, with a long list of waiting hopefuls, Mr Bakshi's father despised them. In deference to his father's sentiment, Mr Bakshi had diverted all of his charity budget to the greater good of the Ram Tirath Hospital.

He had been much more wary of the Sikhs these days, their anger like a crouched leopard ready to leap at the victim. Look at that Balli, behaving like he had been stung by a swarm of bees, showing me his teeth. Must tell my son not to be overfriendly with him, he thought, despite sitting in captivity, uncertain if he would ever walk out a free man and equally uncertain of being able to dictate a friendship list to his son.

✖

And now Balli was walking on the floor that may have been paid for by Mr Bakshi and wondering if he had the moral right to be walking here and if the floor would not recognize treachery in a footstep and trip him up for it. The thought made Balli tread even more carefully even though he recognized his fear as superstition.

At his mother's bedside he became a child again, helpless and uncertain about what to do, a set of ten clumsy thumbs when he was called upon to prop up her pillows or propel a spoonful of milk and cornflakes into her unwilling mouth. He would end up depositing most of her food into her lap instead, and would then get into a flurry of cleaning up with those same ten thumbs.

His mother saw him as a little boy too. Not an unusual circumstance, given the fact that most parents continue to see even their grown-up, grey-haired, rickety-in-the-knees offspring as spring chicken.

Balli was standing by her bedside, all of eight years old, his hair tied into a knot on top of his head, a white hanky covering it and held in place by a rubber band, his knickers hoisted almost up to his chest, in perpetual fear of being found at his ankles instead, since his little drum of a stomach would not provide a waisted niche to the belt. There was an expression of extreme concentration on his face as he held a newborn baby in his arms.

'Your sister,' Inder said to him.

'Ma, see how tiny her hands are,' said Balli, measuring his own against the baby's and feeling like a powerful giant.

'Why are you telling him that?' said Inder's mother-in-law. 'He does not need to know. These things must not be spoken about otherwise they become difficult to do.'

'I am sure he will live with these horrible memories anyway.'

'Only if you put labels on things, find words for them. Let them be like swirling mists which he cannot grasp, then they go away.'

Pigeon logic, thought Inder of her mother-in-law. Shut your eyes and danger goes away. Keep quiet about it and it never happened.

'I have been through the same thing,' said her mother-in-law. 'You will thank me for it. I ruled over the household I was married into because I brought them only sons. Nobody need know the rest.'

Balli, in the absence of his father, was filling in for him as the head of the family, but that did not mean he needed to know everything. His father had gone to Manali. They had tried to tell him that it would be very cold there, that temperatures would be running in the minus range, that it was not the tourist season, that it could even be snowing.

'In fact, it is the tourist season,' said Balli's father.

'The tourist season?' said his wife.

'It is to see the snow that I am going and that is what tourists go there for,' he had said.

'Oh, the snow?' said his wife.

'Yes, the snow. Why do you have to repeat everything I say?'

See the snow indeed, thought his wife. No one ever mentioned the mistress in Manali.

He had left in his Gypsy, the sound of the engine rising from a purr to an urgent frenzy as it reversed out of the drive and quickly merged into the roar of the traffic out on the street. Meanwhile, Inder went into her labour pains.

Balli's grandmother was ready with a jug of cold water, which had been kept on the roof through the freezing December night. But now the sun was struggling with the early morning fog, managing to jab the earth with an occasional ray of light, which was promptly blunted by the unyielding vapour. It was important to get this thing over with before the water became tepid.

Balli had felt very important as he participated in the ceremony. It was like sitting at the head of the table and from that vantage, viewing the rest. He thought it might be a story to tell at school the next day.

It wasn't. You can't tell stories in which you are not a hero. And then it makes better sense to tell it like it happened to someone else. But for that you need the guile of an adult or the craft of a storyteller. Balli had neither guile nor craft, so he never told the story at all. And every story that sits festering, undigested in the stomach, has to be expelled as either diarrhea or vomit, otherwise it multiplies into a thousand little monsters that further sprout many heads, until a whole colony has set up camp inside, the pinnacle of their pitched tent stabbing straight into the heart.

He had watched horrified as his grandmother poured the jug of cold water on the baby—his sister. He could mention this to no one. Not even to himself. The baby, red in the face and howling, had suddenly turned silent and blue in his arms, like litmus paper. In later years, Balli had dropped out of studying sciences because he could not handle the litmus test—turning red when immersed in acid and blue in alkali. The searing red and bloodless blue. He would much rather study geography.

Balli, at eight, thought that he had not behaved like a man. Certainly not worthy of the head of the table, he thought. And as it happened, he was to live with manhood as his most pressing problem. But at eight, he had dumped the baby on his mother and run out of the front door. Out into the garden where the plants were still drenched in the juices of the night. And then to the road.

Parsinni was sent to fetch him. Parsinni, with her sari wrapped tightly around her like a winding sheet, was the ultimate caregiver, with a straying husband and many dead children behind her in Bihar, and a fund of maternal sentiments which she had carried with her when she came to Punjab to offer her services as an ayah.

'Come in Baali baba,' she had said.

'I am not coming in,' he had said. So the two of them had walked up and down on the road as though out for a morning walk.

Inder had watched everything from her bed. It had not taken long. Just a quick dousing out of life with a jug of very cold water. But when Balli had left her holding the dead baby, she had gone into paroxysms of sorrow, tear-filled hiccups that echoed loudly in the room with its high ceiling and rafters. Her mother-in-law had tried to comfort her—telling of her own time, of how these things are always done, and done in a certain way, of how there are traditions to uphold, of how society exerts some pressures, of how some who withstand them and others that don't, succumb, and of how she too would have loved it if her own daughter had lived. She had even cradled her in her arms, expressing an empathy which came from her very guts. But Inder lived silently with the horror of it for the rest of her years.

Now, in this sanitized hospital room, she was looking for an equally quick conclusion to her own life but was instead lingering on the fringes of it. In and out she went. Spotting the actors on the television set in front of her and catching the light in the window when she was conscious of her surroundings; grappling with ghosts and blinded by a surreal glow when she was remembering the horrors of the past. When she did finally die, there were beings, the size of little children, armed with iron hooks, who had beckoned to her soul. 'Come out, come out, we will tear you to pieces.'

11

'Don't try that,' said a booming voice, which seemed to have come straight out of a megaphone, like the voice of god in some tacky television serial. 'We will chop you up and feed you to the dogs. We will throw the morsels out of that very window. No one will know where you went.' An elaborate threat, a detailed recipe for annihilation, not the usual unimaginative 'I will kill you.'

Mr Bakshi had been jangling the window latch in a frenzy. He had noticed the window only a few minutes ago, having been completely focused on the door earlier. It had acquired an overwhelming presence, staring back at him with an unblinking evil eye that obliterated all else. The window was sealed and he now remembered that he had been made to climb stairs. A pistol had prodded him on as he stumbled over the blanket that crowded his feet. He had passed out somewhere in the course of this elaborate procedure but he knew that he was on a first floor, so did he really dare to make that leap? In spite of the possibility of splattering himself all over the road below like a casually spewed paan, the window continued to seem like a tempting escape option and he had gone at the latch with the zeal of a fanatic. He had been caught in the act because he made far too much noise.

'Don't try that,' the voice said yet again.

He had not dared to turn around and look.

The voice had gone on to say that if he knew what was good for him he would not try to escape. Mr Bakshi did feel that it would be an excellent idea for him to try and escape, and very good for him too, but there seemed to be no space for argument with booming, faceless voices.

The voice was on the other side of the door and had obviously heard his attempts at the window.

At that moment he made his god all sorts of promises. He would make a pilgrimage to Vaishno Mata in Jammu. Not once but every year for the next five years. A note made to the heavens above in the deepest possible ink. He did not want to be accused of ingratitude. He would make peace with his wife's family, whom he had not quite forgiven for their many acts of what he saw as negligence and slights towards the importance of his person—amongst others, the gift of a shirt and a necktie on his brother-in-law's wedding. Was he expected to remain naked waist below? Why had they not bothered to present him with an accompanying pair of trousers, he had asked his wife.

I will give up eating meat, he thought. Liquor too. He had never smoked so he was in the clear there. He would even forgive Balli for rattling his teeth, and a man could not promise more than that, there being a natural limit to goodness and tolerance.

He might have been heartened had he known that the owner of the voice was just as scared as he was. But then, sometimes there is very little to distinguish between bravery and fear, between the man who shoots because he is bursting with bravado and the other who pulls the trigger because he is terrified. In fact, the world stored in neat little boxes with appropriate labels pasted on them can easily fall into complete disarray, a messy jumble, when the going gets difficult. The bravery in Gurjant Singh's booming voice was quite questionable, though Mr Bakshi froze on the latch on hearing it. Nor was the size of their penises indicative of much else other than physical dimensions. Or maybe there was something to it—Gurjant Singh with his little one being the subject of much speculation and ministration and Mr Bakshi with his being an unsung appendage and a largely unknown entity—large or small, no one, other than his wife, knew.

In any case, Mr Bakshi became an icicle on the latch and Gurjant Singh was afraid of opening the door because that would necessitate action. He would have to go in with the force of a tornado and generate a whirlwind to frighten the man into submission. He would have to threaten and intimidate. He would have to rave and rant and talk in the venomous low tones of a particularly dangerous, hard-heeled gangster. And today he was just not up to it. After all, a man has to have his moods and moments. It is not the prerogative of the artist only. He thought that he might come back another time, and the ferocity of his voice from behind a closed door might suffice for just now. In any case he had had his fill of coercive action for the day. He had thrown the blanket over Mr Bakshi, encircled his waist and hoisted him into the boot of the vehicle like the tailor did his mannequins at Dhakka Colony. Gurjant had been ably assisted by the rest of his gang. He had followed this up with maniacal driving, screeching and swerving at turns, the vehicle tilting dangerously on two wheels as though for action cinema, because he thought that was the appropriate thing to do, though there was no one giving them chase, and a leisurely pace would have reached them to their destination just as well and more innocuously too. But that might have taken away from the enormity of the occasion and he could not afford to slacken just then. After he had metered a decent distance from the scene of the crime, he had brought Mr Bakshi out of the boot and deposited him on the rear seat and driven out of town and onto village roads. He had to wait for the anonymity of darkness to execute the rest. Mr Bakshi's abduction gear was pared down from a blanket to a blindfold, the transition being effected with the precision of a surgeon who transfers his patient to a heart-lung machine before surgery—not a second unaccounted for in between. Mr Bakshi did not manage even a passing glimpse at his surroundings but found himself stumbling blindly through fields, his ears perked up for giveaway sounds—a tubewell tattooing a tuk tuk tuk in the vicinity, the air vibrating with the sound, a road running in the distance, an occasional horn announcing its presence. But he could not fathom where he was.

Once home, Gurjant had decided that the victim must be kept on the first floor. Up the stairs went Mr Bakshi, Gurjant's hand holding a banana, in imitation of a pistol, digging into the other's back. Gurjant did not want to use the real weapon because, as he explained later to his gang members, he was so quick with it that he feared he might do harm even before their purpose had been achieved. Quick on the draw and quick to anger is how he saw himself. He belonged to Bhatinda, which is the Wild West of Punjab, where it was routine practice to shoot to kill over a land dispute and equally routine to fire shots in the air at a wedding out of sheer, undiluted joy. At Bhatinda, venues for marriage parties posted notices disallowing the carrying of firearms. But this only acted as a greater incentive to not only carry them in, but to also discharge them in the course of the festivities. He belonged to Bhatinda, and had to prove his antecedents, if not in letter, then at least in spirit. The banana, therefore, butted into Mr Bakshi's back in keeping with this spirit.

However, they were all quite unclear about this aforesaid 'purpose'. What did they really want? They could not want a Khālistān, a nation of Sikhs. The demand had very nearly gone out of circulation, though it was a suggestion that had surfaced from as far back as the forties, then again in the sixties, the seventies, the eighties—like a well-timed chime. It appeared as a pamphlet in the forties, which saw Khālistān as a buffer state between India and Pakistan; as a political conference in the sixties, which felt that Sikhs had been wronged and were left with no alternative but to ask for self determination; as a resolution in the seventies, which asked for autonomy; and as an agitation in the eighties, which turned to violence. At roadside kiosks posters of the now dead Sant Jarnail Singh Bhindranwale, big daddy of the insurgent movement of the eighties, were displayed carelessly next to those of film stars. Dream girl Hema Malini, her kohled eyes awash with emotion, looking out of one poster while he, his eyes fierce and combative, looked out of another. The demand had since mellowed into a series of jokes—about Khalistani currency, about the national bird of Khālistān, about political parties, all of them playing upon the Punjabi love for good food and bravado, sometimes mindless, sometimes exemplary.

A landlocked nation, some had said, how could it be practical?

'Sardar Sahib, it is not as though we are looking to catch

fish, we are seeking to create a nation,' the enthusiasts had said to these sceptics.

But Gurjant Singh and Co. did not have it that well worked out. They knew they had to have some demand. Any demand. A kidnapping without aim would only be like making wild sword stabs in the air. A demand for money would have made them look like mercenaries, which they were not, they told themselves. They were warriors of the guru. They were his representatives here on earth, bananas and all. Not bandits. The sheen of the Khālistān had to be preserved.

They had discussed it among themselves. In fact, they had discussed it over several rounds of desi liquor. It had made them smell like a freshly dressed wound, that has been cleaned with spirit. They were drinking santri, and though the name suggested an orangey flavour, there was no such subtlety to it. It was a quicky whisky, ready in a jiffy. Molasses from sugar-cane factories fermented into spirit brought to the right proof and distilled, and in two days the whisky was ready. No cellars, no barrels, no bottling dates, no issues of antiquity. It could be called anything from santri to gabru to jugni, from flavours, to youthfulness, to femininity. The names did not really matter to them. The headiness did. It could have been santri or gabru when it came to whisky and Mr Bakshi or Mr Bansal could be their kidnap victims. Names were inconsequential; it was the potency that mattered.

And so they discussed the matter at hand. In the evening they sat in the courtyard of Jagjit Singh Khalsa's house and hoped to draw some inspiration from the man himself. He was no ordinary seventy-six-year-old. A saffron turban clumsily tied, one fold coming unstuck at the back like a tendril shyly peeping out of a lush growth, an array of medals decorating his breast, slung from his neck with satin ribbons. His bushy, white eyebrows hung over his eyes like twin awnings and his white beard cascaded down to his waist. He had retired at the age of fifty-eight as the headmaster of a school, where he had rattled off rules on participles and gerunds and articles at a motorized pace, pausing only occasionally for breath. At sixty he had taken to cycling. He cycled two hundred and fifty kilometres everyday. To Delhi and back, to Bombay and back. Twelve hours to Delhi. Seven days to Bombay. And back. Nothing was a one-way ride. To get a visa for Canada, he had cycled all the way to Delhi and was then told that he would get it much closer home in Jalandhar. He had not baulked, but simply turned his cycle around and cycled back. 'Like a cow,' was how he described himself; 'whichever direction my face is turned, I just go.'

In the old days he had neither beard nor turban, but this new awakening to religion had come, he said, as 'a call from a voice within', though admittedly there were many external voices around saying similar things—things about justice and its travesty and the necessity to adhere to religious practices, with the specific intention of countering a perceived threat to the identity of the Sikhs.

'They don't want Punjab to come forward,' he used to say.

'They? Who?'

If someone asked him, he usually fumbled and thought and said, 'these Madrasis and Bungalis'—those Indians south of the Vindhya Mountains for whom the Punjabis nurtured a healthy contempt. They all came under the broad rubric of 'Madrasis' and 'Bungalis', and it did not matter in the least what Indian state they actually belonged to.

His impressive command over the English language

combined with his physical prowess made him something of an icon. Gurjant Singh and his men always took his words very seriously, particularly when they were spoken in English. Jagjit Singh translated his own verbose English into Punjabi for their benefit.

Now he pumped air into his cycle tyres preparing for his daily odyssey, which would begin at four in the morning, and said in his most floral Punjabi, 'The flower of Punjab's youth, this immense fund of talent is rotting today. And all because of these people.'

That made Gurjant and Co. feel even more persecuted. After all, they were the youth of Punjab and they had to have talent even though they did not quite see themselves as flowers. In any case, Punjabis always think that there is a plot against them. And this sense of grievance gave the kidnapping a lofty purpose.

'I will tell you what we will do,' said Gurjant. He had suddenly become a man with a plan and he was not the gang leader for nothing. Bhola, the innocence of his name inbuilt into his character quite by chance, had suggested that they ask for Chandigarh in lieu of Mr Bakshi.

'Chandigarh should be made a part of Punjab, its capital. After all, they did not give us a Khālistān. At least our state should be given something.'

'Don't be an innocent.' Gurjant had slapped his back in remonstrance. 'You really think they will do that? Give you Chandigarh indeed! They would rather bomb it out of existence than give it to you. And even so, you are not the guy they will give it to, even if you happen to be the last and only man on this earth. You really have an inflated notion of yourself.'

Jawaharlal Nehru had commissioned the building of the city on a flat piece of land, with picturesque hills providing the background. The prime minister had periodically surveyed its progress from a tall tower erected at the heart of the site for this very purpose. The city was an in vitro fertilization, one that sprang out of the lines on a drawing board, an immaculate conception, quite unlike the birth of Ludhiana. Why does everyone have to covet it so much, Gurjant wondered. He had no great love for the city, but when everyone else clamoured for it and listed its denial as one of the many grievances of the Sikh community against the Central Government, he had thought fit to join the chorus. Personally though, he would much rather live in the winding lanes of Ludhiana than in the straight line geometry of Chandigarh. The interstices in Ludhiana allowed for much, for a jhaat, a peek-a-boo, a surprise confrontation, or a secret tucked away, including the stashing away of Mr Bakshi.

And poor Mr Bakshi was feeling like a very well-kept secret indeed. Stashed away, waiting to be transported, he did not know where. Maybe the hereafter, he thought, and that sent a tremor down his spine. He would have been very nervous had he known that he had very nearly become a pawn on the negotiating table to be bartered away for Chandigarh. Men had died before this for staking claim to the city. Darshan Singh Pheruman had fasted in 1969 and died after seventy-four days. He had soon been forgotten. Other leaders, like Sant Fateh Singh, it was rumoured, had pretended to fast, consuming, behind the scenes and in the privacy of night, large dollops of kada parshad, which can be a whole meal in itself—flour, generous quantities of rarified butter and sugar. Certainly an indulgence which would not let anyone die of starvation. The parshad being an offering in a gurdwara also ensured that a sense of virtuousness prevailed over the guilt of having cheated. Neither fasting nor feasting succeeded. No one got Chandigarh. Neither Punjab, nor the neighbouring state of Haryana. The Union Territory came to stand for all that was desirable and yet elusive—wooed by all, giving herself to none.

Bhola had no use for Chandigarh. He had never even been there, but he thought that since his companions were looking around for a cause, this one may just be as good as any other. So, it was in a moment of inspiration that he had suggested Chandigarh. After shooting it down, Gurjant had said, 'I will tell you what we will do. We will let them know that we have done it just to show them what we can do. We will not ask for anything. We will tell them "you bugger us, we will bugger you."'

'Then there is nothing that we want in return for Bakshi? We just return him?' asked one of the gang.

That confused Gurjant a little. But leadership requires decisiveness.

'We keep him,' he said, terse and to the point.

'Keep him?' said the others. 'Forever?'

These questions about eternity are always tricky because they force you to think not just about the immediate in that they project the present into a distant future. Eternity is a long haul. For instance, the query made Gurjant picture Mr Bakshi in that barricaded first floor room in Sunet for the next five years—even the exigency of a forever could not force him to go beyond five. Five was phenomenal enough. There he was, five years later, handing rolled rotis to his prisoner, through a crack in the door, morning and evening. Keeping him alive and yet not quite. Playing hide-and-seek with the police, locking up and leaving the house and then coming back to check if he had forgotten to lock up. Tugging at the locked lock and then feeling foolish. Looking around to see that no one had seen.

'I meant that we keep him and then send him on to eternity,' he said, issuing a clarification with that meaningful look, pretending that that was what he had indicated all along, even though he had only just thought of the amendment.

Mr Bakshi was a fly in his throat he could neither swallow nor spit.

The fly now stepped away from the window and desisted from any further rattling of the latch. Mr Bakshi spent the night working out his opening lines and preparing to pronounce his considered opinion when the door did open, because hunger and fear would not let him sleep.

Gurjant heaved a tired sigh of resignation on the other side of the door early the next morning, and decided that he might as well go in. There was really no point in putting off the moment, after all an artist is also sometimes required to push himself beyond the vagaries of whimsicality. He had tucked a hanky behind his ears to cover his mouth and nose and sharpened the look in his eyes for added effect. He was ready to display his belligerence to his victim, who would by now be considerably disabled with hunger. He pushed open the door, expecting supplication, grovelling, a drool of emotion, a drivel of fear. But he was not prepared for a fusillade of English.

'Today the world is in the phase of ignorance, darkness, greediness, selfishness, theftness, bribeness and moreover the corruption,' said Mr Bakshi in his most studied English, hoping that the weightiness of his words would intimidate and then sink the scales in his favour. It worked quite to the contrary on both counts.

Gurjant was open-mouthed for a moment. Only for a moment though. Then his aggression surged back. Luckily for Mr Bakshi, Gurjant had not understood a word.

But it did give Gurjant an opportunity to make a point. 'Why can't you speak Punjabi?' he said. 'You think your moustache goes up a fraction just because you speak like a yankee?' He was of course talking of a metaphorical moustache since Mr Bakshi did not have any, or only as much as accrues overnight—a tired suggestion of stubble. As it was, it could not have stood in for a symbol of pride.

Gurjant gripped him by the shoulders and shook him into a blur, both for the English that he spoke, which Gurjant would be quite glad to have been able to speak himself, and for the necessity of frightening him into submission. He succeeded in sending Mr Bakshi into a terrified tremble.

'Cold, are you?' said Gurjant, dripping sarcasm while Mr Bakshi was dripping sweat. 'Poor you. Let me wrap you in this blanket and make you cosy.'

It was a red hot day, the blinding white sunlight had made everything hissing hot. Blankets should have been stored away with moth balls for the summer, but this blanket seemed to have become Mr Bakshi's preferred attire.

That English was a mistake, he thought, his brain having been tossed around into a confused jumble of short-circuited wires, which were now melting in the heat.

'I am hungry,' he said, the lines from his stomach to his head still in place.

'Then say that, instead of that long, fancy speech you just gave.'

Gurjant called downstairs for alu paranthas. Bhola quickly scampered across to the dhaba where the 'boys', as Gurjant Singh and Co. were known in the neighbourhood, had a running account, and brought back two wrapped in a newspaper.

Two rolled rotis, thought Gurjant with a sinking sense of dèjá vu, as he handed them over to Mr Bakshi.

12

Sweety was eating with gusto. The night before had been particularly trying. It was difficult to eat a meal with all those drunks on the loose at marriage parties. She had danced till she felt as though she would have dropped dead with fatigue and hunger. The dinner spread had been three hundred dishes. Could have been more, not less. She had only rounded off the figure in her head. She had served herself things with strange names. Kai yakitori and dragon roll, amidst the more familiar alu lajawaab and bhindi kurkuri. She had tried asking the waiters stationed behind the groaning tables. Kai yakitori? But they had only smirked, whether at her or at the yakitori, she did not know. She had decided to be adventurous, to stare down the smirks and yakitori, and to tango with the unknown. But overtures from men who had watched her dance followed her around like a primeval curse that is difficult to shake off. She had opted to give up her plate instead.

In the morning she woke up to the exposition of a raga in her stomach, the notes flowing freely but tending to the single theme of hunger. She got up and made herself a parantha in the makeshift kitchen in the corner of her room.

She was eating when Gurjant came in.

'Be a brother and just scratch my back for me,' she said as she licked her fingers clean.

Gurjant did not feel brotherly at all but obliged nevertheless.

'Just a little to the right,' she said, her eyes closed. 'Lower… no no…that is too low…higher…a little left…yes, just there… go on…keep going…don't stop…hmmmm…hmmmmm…'

The ecstasy of being scratched at just that right spot was an unmatched sensation, thought Sweety. Unmatched yes, but then there were those others. The moment of orgasm, for instance. That was good too, a soaring of senses aboard a jetliner, when issues of sexual morality and survival became but miniatures in the distance down below. But then, it was followed by a feeling of emptiness. Back scratching had no such falling out.

'Hmmmm,' she said again.

'How long?' said Gurjant, his patience wearing thin.

'Already tired? Alright, you can stop.'

Gurjant had come to propose to Sweety, not to scratch her back. It might have been different if she too had scratched his back but then that would have needed a different idiom, the English one, to be applicable. He felt that she might see him in a different light now that he had been man enough to show his muscle. He had Mr Bakshi in custody and was on the verge of making his point to the world at large, even though the point itself was slightly hazy in his head.

His hangers-on had advised him against marriage and particularly to Sweety. You can barely keep yourself going and here you are, thinking about marriage—they had said in varying ways. They had even advised him to place a demand for money as ransom for the release of Mr Bakshi. 'We could set up a chain ransom,' said one of them. 'This cartoon could give us the name of another rich seth whom we could then kidnap. And then, that one in turn could give us the name of yet another one. And we could just build it up like that.' It sounded like a business venture that was bound to grow. 'Two lakh from each and that should keep us going fairly well.' It was a calculation in which imponderables did not exist. No police, no state machinery, no enforcement of law and order, not even an angry, vigilant, retaliatory public. Just a fairy-tale world in which the thief thieves and saunters away with riches.

'And why marry? Why marry someone who has seen it all already? Seen the ups and downs of it all?' They had said it crudely but then that was man to man and he did not mind. What he did mind though, was Sweety addressing him as 'brother'.

'By God,' she said. 'I was really hungry.'

'They did not give you any food last night?' he asked her.

'There was enough food to feed all of Dhakka Colony for one week,' she said indignantly, but wondering all the while why she was taking their part in this exchange. But Gurjant and she were naturally antithetical—two swords in one scabbard. They had to fight. If he had said something about how hot it was, she probably would have contested it, even though the sweat stood in stubborn beads on her forehead.

'Just so, and yet they did not give you any food,' he said, teasing her.

'I chose not to eat,' she said haughtily.

The teasing was not really teasing. It was a mating call.

He did not like her profession even though he was seduced by it in a subterranean sort of way—pornography in his pyjamas, piousness in his pants.

'Why can't you do something else?' he said, invoking the commandment from the insurgents that proscribed dancing.

'Maybe they will employ me as the chief minister,' she said sweetly.

The state was in need of a chief minister just then. The one it had was blown away by a bomb outside the secretariat in Chandigarh. Forensic experts were left picking up the pieces, though in strictly physical terms there was not very much to pick up. A shoe which belonged to the assassin. An assortment of limbs. Mangled metal. Glass shards. The chief minister had disappeared into thin air. There were no remains to make up even a handful for an urn. In later years, the government would try to remedy that by providing a plot of land where a memorial would serve in place of the ashes that had blown away with the pernicious wind. The assassin, a disgruntled policeman in uniform, had worn gelatin sticks under his belt and when he blew himself up, triggered by a nine-volt battery, the sound echoed back into town from the mountains in the background. Insurgency had been quelled a few years ago, but did this announce another beginning, or just a last convulsion, an echo?

'If you marry me you might become important enough for them to consider the option,' he told her, pretending to be facetious but secretly savouring the headlines that he would make.

His predecessors in the insurgent movement had been even more conscious of the headlines and the image. One of them was known to measure the length of exposed forehead with the markings on his forefinger to make sure that his turban sat symmetrically on his head. Gurjant was only keeping up yet another tradition.

'Haan, yes,' she said, playing along with the charade of his pre-eminence, 'maybe they will make you the chief minister and I can be the first lady.' Then she paused and said, 'No, I don't want to marry you.'

'Don't want to marry me?'

'Don't want to marry you.' The repetition gave each some time to mull over the next move.

'I wouldn't marry you even if you were the last man on earth.'

That changed the tone of the exchange from friendly parrying to viciousness. If they were going to trade insults, then he was pretty good at it himself. He could give her as good as he got.

'Are you going to die an old maid then? Who is going to marry you? You don't know a good thing when you see it.'

If Gurjant was the 'good thing' in Sweety's life then there had obviously been some kind of reallocation of the values of good and bad since last she knew of it. They circled each other warily like opponents in a kabbadi match. She wanted to make the home run, and decided to have it out with him.

'Why? Why would I die an old maid? Only a few months ago a man had come with a proposal. Kailla, I think his name was. And he told me that someone in that white kothi of the big sardars had seen me and liked me.'

'Aho, one of those sardars will marry you, will they? They will only make you dance some more in those silly skirts of yours. You look like a fairy doll in a salwaar kameez but in these skirts…you look a karaant.' To Gurjant, a skirt looked like an uncomfortable attempt at being English and Christian.

In the general hierarchy of acceptance, to be English was something to be looked up to but to be Indian Christian was to be looked down upon. The antipathy ran far into the past, from as far back as the nineteenth century when Ludhiana became the centre of Christian missionary activities. The missionaries were seen as the stooges of the British. However, their methods of evangelization were grudgingly admired by the Hindu Arya Samajis and Sikh Singh Sabha. The missionaries had set up the first Punjabi printing press, admittedly for their own ends, but while they churned out publications on Christianity, Punjabi prose developed as a by-product. There was even a Punjabi phonetic reader that lay open under a glass case in the Punjabi Bhawan library. *1914*, by T. Grahame Bailey, MA, BD, Fellow of the Punjab University, University of London Press, London. Punjabi pronunciation made easy by an Englishman! However, 'karaant' was neither literary, nor Punjabi, nor a phonetic feat. It was just the result of an ancient, epileptic anger that had contorted speech. Karaant for Christian. The anger was now forgotten history but the distortion had become part of the vocabulary, not without a value judgement though.

Gurjant's own history was quite illustrious. Not the kind that fetches public accolades, nor merits a photograph in a gallery of heroes, but it was certainly worth a telling. His great-grandfather hadn't died playing at home with his grandchildren. He had died with his boots on, literally. Over a century ago he had marched into Ludhiana on the ninth of June, riding on the wave of the 1857 mutiny against the British. Boots and breeches and bravado. His moustaches pointing fingers at the sky. His spirits pitched even beyond. He had come in with the other mutineers, though they said that most Sikhs were supporting the British, and by that logic, he really was on the wrong side of things. He had made straight for the fort, the same fort that was now like a set of teeth infested with cavities. It was not so then. It was a stronghold from where power emanated. The aspiring nationalists had mounted and manned their guns at the fort and were in a fair way to giving the British a run for their money, the one they had made out of Indian sweat. In that moment of triumph, Gurjant's great-grandfather discovered that he had carried with him blank cartridges instead of balled cartridges, his firepower being reduced to merely the fire that he carried in his head. His looks could then kill but his guns would not. That had briefly taken the shine out of the moment but his natural buoyancy had bobbed him up once again, as he made ready to march on to Delhi along with the others. But an unarmed man is bound to fall to the enemy bullet. And he did. In hindsight, had they stayed on and consolidated their position at the fort, the British would have lost this very important city—which lay on the high road to Delhi—and history might have taken a different course.

Maybe Gurjant's propensity to carry unloaded weaponry, subsequently substituted by bananas, took root way back then, as also the inclination to slip off the high road into the sidings of parody.

He tended to provoke more laughter than tears, even though his intent was otherwise. And whatever the provocation, historical or immediate, Gurjant did not like skirts. Dark hair and dark legs were only karaant. Awkward legs sticking out from under a swirl of material. Legs, which did not know what to do with themselves. Should they be crossed or demure, placed side by side with knees knocking against each other?

'And have you ever seen your mug?' she asked him, raising the pitch yet another notch, of both temperature and volume, as also of physiology, her hand pointing to his face to shift the focus away from her legs and onto his physiognomy.

She, too, was uncomfortable in those skirts but she was not going to admit it and certainly not to Gurjant. She might as well let him have it—above the belt, below the belt, wherever. The argument spiralled its way upwards, like steam from an angrily boiling kettle.

'Why, what is wrong with it?' he asked, thrusting his face at her.

'Uuhah,' she said, simulating a vomit.

That made him ballistic. The neighbours gathered outside. Time for a fight. It had been a long time. And a fight always cleared the air. Everyone went home, spent and satisfied. It worked on the principle of a homeopathic cure. Bring out all the poison, let there be the sudden eruptions of a million sores, festering and weeping, clearing the system and skin after it had all been expended.

Gurjant was rocketing along on a reckless anger, saying and doing things that he would later wish he had not done or said.

'Bitch, whore, bastard woman, fat-arsed buffalo, black witch,' he rattled off. As he ran out of expletives that would be specific to women, he launched into the usual sisterfucker, motherfucker and daughterfucker tirade even though they crossed the gender divide and were employed more as pause and punctuation by vehement Punjabi speakers.

He did not regret the fact that he had gone on from her to the rest of her family, to her father, her mother, her sisters and brothers, abusing them with heartfelt venom even though he did not know any of them. He did not regret having stamped around furiously like a particularly vigorous kathak dancer in an ecstasy of creativity, smoke emanating from all his orifices.

Nor did he regret having flung a few things around, amongst them the little clay animals that he had bought for her, a red-beaked parrot, an open-mouthed bird, a plumaged peacock, a cavorting horse, well-fed bullocks—all of them in the colours of embroidered phulkari—explosive pink, dirty yellow, bright green, since the craftsmen who had fashioned them were not aspiring for verisimilitude. They were trying to capture the vibrancy of spirit. He had bought them at Bhagtu da Mela in Khatkar Kalan, at the fair in memory of Shaheed Bhagat Singh, who had been hanged by the British. This was an annual pilgrimage for him, an hour's bus ride from Ludhiana. Gurjant would visit the martyr's ancestral home, a small unassuming structure, forlorn looking—an indifferent whitewash hiding its original brick construction. There was a visitors book that was a hand down from a snack bar at the Wagah border, with an entry in it that said, 'The family of a martyr should be given due respect, which seems to be still due.' Gurjant would then go to the museum and stare yet again at Bhagat Singh's entry on the second page of the diary issued to him in jail—'lovers, lunatics and poets are made of the same stuff'. He would breathe deeply, inhale the ambience of revolt, of a reckless madness, and a voice in his head would say—'Keep your distance, I am Bhagat Singh'. It made him feel important. He would go out suffused with determination to fight the Indian state even though Bhagat Singh had died fighting for it. That having been done he would loiter about in the grounds and survey the stalls with the air of a dignitary taking a salute from assembled contingents. Ultimately he would buy knick-knacks, eat candy floss that had materialized like a spiderweb in the wheel that was spun by the candy-floss man, and be back on the bus by the evening.

Those keepsakes from Khatkar Kalan now lay around with broken necks and fractured legs. He was also pleased at having broken the only other piece of decoration—the glass paperweight in which colourful specks had danced around and which had sat blinking on the only table in her room.

But he did wish that he had not given her the entire lowdown on his activities in a voice that could be heard down the road. He wished that he had been a little more circumspect. He wished that he had not boasted. In short, he wished that he had not told her of Mr Bakshi going molten in a room upstairs in Sunet. And particularly, that he had not told her in a voice loud enough to be heard by the neighbourhood.

She did not take it very well. In fact, it was her turn to be furious.

13

Two days later, very early in the morning, at one of those hours when it is not quite morning and not really night, when late risers have just begun to get a good night's sleep and early risers were springing out of bed in readiness for the day, the police were standing outside the double-storey structure in Sunet. A truckload of them had descended and fanned out—sultry, khaki lines of surly policemen, the long arm of the law. It was a cordon and search operation. Sources said a man had claimed to have kidnapped the industrialist Bakshi. The news had made headlines in local newspapers: 'Bakshi of Bakshi & Bakshi Enterprises Blindfolded and Bundled away', 'Terror Revisited, Bakshi Abducted'.

'Sources' was an ubiquitous entity that worked both for the police and journalists. 'According to sources...' said the journalists, and that could mean anything, from an actual source of information, to a stray remark by someone at a dinner party or a personal theory pulled out of a fertile brain.

Perhaps it was Sweety. She had been humouring Gurjant all along only because he had seemed harmless—even though he wore jeans a few sizes too tight and moved around with a stiffly starched, deliberate gait that carried him more sideways than forward, was curt when spoken to because it did not behove a *real* man to be soft and pliant, whose repertoire of jokes was limited to the age-old one about the Punjabi athlete Milkha Singh. ('Are you relax-ing? No, I am Milkha Singh.) Gurjant was usually the only one to laugh at this antiquated joke while others wore polite smiles as they heard this one through for the three hundred and fifty-fifth time. His banter included exposing the underside of his shoe, saying 'look into a mirror'. He had grown up in some ways and not in others. But he had also been gentle and responsive to her needs. We all have a dark side, reflected Sweety, but just how dark is dark? It is an internally installed metre that measures umbras and penumbras, the shadows and half shadows. Each metre, a different brand, with different readings.

Maybe she had wrapped herself in an anonymous veil and gone to the police to tell them of the whereabouts of the missing industrialist.

Perhaps it was that man who wore his visor in reverse, always lurking about in the streets, a mukhbir, an informer, a 'cat', as the police liked to call them, because they were expected to be feline and quietly make their way to listening posts. Maybe he had waited for the evening and then cycled to another part of town, to a cigarette kiosk where he pretended to buy cigarettes. 'King of spades,' he had told Roshanlal the vendor, letting drop the code, even as Roshanlal handed him cigarettes from his perch. Or he went to a dhaba where the serving chhotu not only took his order for a tandoori roti and dal but also took the note that he handed to him in such an overtly surreptitious manner that anyone with half an eye would have noticed. Or he asked for fifty kilos of atta to be delivered to his house the next morning from a grocery store.

The verbal messages, or a note, or a sign would be picked up by another man who would then pass it further on, and after a circuitous route devised to hide and jumble its footprints, would arrive at the doorstep of the police. Ultimately someone would contact the man with the visor in reverse and he would tell them all that he saw and heard at Dhakka Colony. A car with darkened windows would take him around town to identify the said man. 'There he is,' he would say, as he spotted Gurjant shading his eyes from the sunlight outside on the road. And then the police would be on Gurjant's tail, following him to the miracle man, perhaps for a second dose of those little globules, to the Subhani building which was threatening to fall on the next visitor's head, to the old clock tower strangulated by a flyover under construction and then finally to Sunet.

In any case, whatever their means of gathering the information, two days after Gurjant proposed to Sweety, the police were there in Sunet.

Gurjant had claimed that he had had a premonition. He had not told his gang that he had lost his cool and spilled all, practically on the street. He had tried to warn his fellow conspirators to make a run for it, citing the instance of his third eye, which not all of them took seriously since this was the first time it had made an appearance.

'A third eye? What is that? Like Lord Shiva's third eye?' they asked him.

He did not want to be seen as alluding to the Hindu pantheon for an analogy and suggested that it was Maharaja Ranjit Singh's eye—the Lion of Punjab, who had consolidated the first Sikh empire in the nineteenth century. Though blind in one eye, the maharaja's one good eye had come to stand for the dispensation of justice.

'But he had only one eye,' said Gurjant's hangers-on, 'and you are talking of a third one.'

'Go fall into a well then, go to hell,' said an irritated Gurjant.

When the police knocked on the door, they had expected to find the ring leader and his entire set of angry young men asleep in their underwear in the summer heat. Not a pretty picture, but very sharply etched in SHO Bachitter Singh's head. Repulsive, he thought, shaking his head, trying to dislodge the image. Hirsute men, unguardedly displaying the remnants of their ancient ancestry. Hairy apes! Why couldn't it be women kidnappers, at least that would make the cat and mouse game a lot more interesting. Imagine discovering an entire contingent of women in nothing but their stringy undergarments. The SHO was momentarily overcome by a surge of fevered fantasy. But then, better to come up against men in a state of undress than to have them sitting all primed and ready with their weapons, waiting for the police to enter. The same police informers could sometimes be informing the other sides. Double agents on a double stipend earning double roti. That kind of thing could put both sides in a fix since both thought they knew what the other was doing.

The police had to break open the lock. Constable Ram Singh was instructed by SHO Bachitter Singh to hammer down the lock with a brick. They had been prepared for a bolt on the inside but not a lock on the outside, which is why they had to resort to slightly archaic methods. The others had stood looking on, their AK-47s ready and pointed. The first brick lying handy on the sidewalk had turned into powder against the door.

'These damn brick kilns and these damn building

contractors,' said Constable Ram Singh as he looked at his hand clutching at red dust. 'Sisterfucker.'

He had been through many such operations and had acquired quite a formidable reputation, which is why he had to be the first one in, though he was no longer very keen on this kind of action. He had won no medals for it. It was mostly brickbats. Not for him personally, but for the police as a whole. Anyone would think that they were remorseless, heartless, flesh-eating vultures. Though, admittedly, that is exactly how he too saw SHO Bachitter Singh, with his peculiar talent for squeezing money out of even the most dehydrated situations—money trickling in from the roadside vendor, the cycle rickshaw man, the garbage collector—the notes browning and limp, soiled with the sweat of their labour. But as SHO Bachitter Singh said, every drop counts. That trickle had built him a house in Model Town, right next to a nascent market. Well-known companies were offering fancy prices to buy him out and build fancy showrooms. But he was proud of his tall house, more vertical than horizontal, and did not want to part with it, even though he was gradually being dwarfed by the giants that were rearing their heads around him.

'Are you going to take all day?' shouted Singh, waking up from his daydream of gun-toting women dressed in underwear, and wanting to blame someone else for it. Constable Ram Singh was a subordinate and available, which made it just so easy.

It was with a sense of peevishness that Constable Ram Singh finally unhinged the lock with a spanner. He makes the dirty money and I have to do the dirty work, he thought.

They went in ready for battle, sticking to the drill on storming a hideout. They tiptoed, took cover, challenged sounds, ran a questioning eye over a room before entering it. But they need not have bothered. There was absolutely no one inside. Not on the ground floor, nor on the second floor. There was only hot air from the flurry of sudden departure.

The kidnappers had also left behind Mr Bakshi tied to his bed. Though he too had once been a lot of hot air, the last two days had beaten all of it out of him. They left him behind because they were all scattering in different directions like a casually thrown handful of marbles. No one wanted Mr Bakshi.

'You take him with you.'

'Why me? He is all yours.'

It had taken them a day to realize the gravity of Gurjant's warning, and that left them only a day to take on other identities, to become one among the many. Lugging Mr Bakshi around as baggage would only have been like wearing an overcoat on a hot summer afternoon and trying to melt into the populace.

They passed the parcel, nobody wanting to be caught with it when the music stopped, or, in this case, started. Finally everyone decided that this hot potato belonged to Gurjant.

'You keep him. You said we had to keep him forever.'

From a cohesive group that spoke in one voice at public forums, they were suddenly many voices at cross purposes. Good times had kept them together, bad times sent them at each other's throat.

'I meant all of us. He is not my uncle. Why would I want to take him along?'

That decided it. Mr Bakshi stayed where he was. All trussed up and nowhere to go.

✶

From Sunet, Gurjant went everywhere. To the UK, the US, Thailand, Nepal, Pakistan. Having evaded arrest once, he subsequently went in and out of jails in different countries. His fate seemed to follow him around like a bad debt. He wondered if someone up there was keeping an account, that too, one that overlooked his serious commitment to religion. It was in the absence of this finer detail in the heavenly account that he was handed out such severe tribulations, he thought.

His travails had begun at Kathmandu, where he had shared a room with four others on the first floor of a guest house. Somebody had sloshed a bucket of water from the balcony. It fell on a guard standing below and the police came and arrested Gurjant. When he got out of that one and reached the US, he was deported very quickly, after doing time in jail there. On the flight back he managed to convince an American woman—his first success at persuasion—in English that was more gesture than speech, that he was likely to be killed the minute he deplaned at Delhi. The woman was suitably horrified and immediately willing to believe the worst of these brown-skinned people with their record of human rights violations. She helped him disembark in Thailand and then on he went to Pakistan. From there he somehow made his way to the UK.

While in Ludhiana his must-carries had included a banana, which he ate before finally leaving on a false passport. He had substituted it with boiled eggs when he was on the run because they offered easy-to-carry sustenance and in any case, his days of threatening people were over, so the banana was quite redundant as a weapon. He had bought the boiled eggs off a street vendor near the railway station, who kept water on the boil and had handed him a dozen of them, along with a generous measure of salt in a pudee—the newspaper scrap cleverly folded many times over to ensure not even a pinch spilled into his pocket.

In all those other lands his pocket also contained a letter from a Khalistani organization certifying him as a member which stated that he was likely to face persecution if he went back to India. He had got the letter and funds from an underground organization. It was underground in more ways than one, since it also operated out of a basement. It employed people who could cook up weepy or gory life stories, depending upon the requirement of the client. Gurjant's letter contained a hair-raising account of his life. From the sound of it, he had been in the forefront of a medieval battle in which his family had been picked up by the police, tortured and raped, he himself subjected to the unheard of, including being pissed upon by a whole police contingent, and then buggered by the same force, and all because he was fighting for the creation of a nation which rightfully belonged to the Sikhs. These stories were not entirely fanciful, they were known to have happened to some and the authors of these stories had merely picked up things from here and there and woven them into a heart-rending narrative.

He thought it sounded better than his own life and that if he had to find asylum in one of these countries, he did need to believe his own story before he could expect others to do so, particularly lawyers and judges. 'My sister was raped before my very eyes and now I have no idea where my entire family is. The police took them away and I have no news of them. I was hung upside down for days together, they pissed and spat on me. I was stretched from both ends till I thought I would break into two halves, like those volunteers at magic shows whom the magician slices into two and puts together again.' This last simile was his own invention and he used it when called upon to narrate his tale. The letter only kept to the sequence of events and did not dabble with things literary. However, his narration was so like a recitation of numerical tables that no one was ever moved. He continued to be an illegal with a letter in his pocket and diminishing hope in his heart.

14

Only mice, thought the policemen. The kind of mice that became emboldened with time spent in human company, sitting on their haunches and staring back with the insolence of a spoilt child, quite at home in the kitchen and drawing room and willing to challenge anyone who might want to evict them. The dull sound of scratching, cutting and sawing came through, breaking silences between whispered words.

The policemen had begun to loosen up after the stress of the past few hours and conversation had gradually risen from nervous whispers to a volume more appropriate for a political rally.

When the grating orchestra of the so-called mice would not be frightened into submissive silence, and in fact, swelled into a deeper layer of resonance, SHO Bachitter Singh said to Constable Ram Singh, 'What is that? Go and see.'

It had to be done through the proper channel because that is how governments function, in a chain of hierarchy that must not be broken. It is a hierarchy behind which the meek and timid can hide and yet hold their heads up high as natural superiors.

'Motherfucker,' said Constable Ram Singh in his head, but went nevertheless, programmed to obey.

And that is how they had found Mr Bakshi, a dead man in his winding sheet. He was not really dead though he looked so. The room was strewn with dead moths' wings, from moths that had winged their way to the single light bulb that burned in the room and singed themselves to death. The light had been a parting kindness, an act of generosity on the part of Gurjant. 'Here, I am leaving this light on so that they will find you.'

There was no response. There could be none since they had stuffed Mr Bakshi's mouth with an underturban. 'Now let me hear you say something in English,' said Gurjant, as his last throwaway line.

'Gggggg' said Mr Bakshi, from the many folds of the underturban. But by then Gurjant had already gone. He was still saying 'ggggg' when they finally found him.

Over the two months of imprisonment before Gurjant had spilled the beans to Sweety, Mr Bakshi had become a lizard on the wall, his ear pressed against it, trying to absorb some of its cool while everything else burned hot. He would listen to sounds and anticipate footsteps, and work out in his mind whether those footsteps meant trouble or food or both. 'Wrong again' or 'right again and that makes twelve rights against eight wrongs, I won, I won'. That is how he kept his sanity, in an insane sort of way. Because when the world is standing on its head, it may just be a good idea to do likewise. He would count cows in his head, go over his life inch by eventful inch, saying and doing the things he had already said and done in a dramatic recreation of the past, and pretend that it was only a question of marking time, of putting it in reverse gear and that the world would right itself in the end, like it had so many times before. Mountains could be moved, he believed. As a four-year-old he could remember going to Murree, and as they circled their way up the hills from Rawalpindi, his insides heaving, he had told his father to remove the mountain. 'The same one keeps coming again and again, just take it away,' he had said in exasperation. As an adult he had continued to believe that mountains could be moved, even if only metaphorically.

But that was before he was tied to the bed, almost becoming one with the weave of the cot, the same tape that made up its warp and weft wrapped around his prone body.

'Gggggggggggggggg,' he said, his verbosity severely curtailed by the awkwardness of talking with a full mouth. Constable Ram Singh heard him from the other side of the door, which had been concealed by an ornamental wooden cupboard stationed right there. It was pushed aside to reveal yet another locked door.

'Panna,' said Constable Ram Singh, in the manner of a surgeon demanding his instruments from a compliant nurse.

The requisition was handed down the hierarchy. The bottom of the heap scurried downstairs for the spanner that had been abandoned there and handed it to Constable Ram Singh. He broke into the room. They had missed this locked door earlier. The emptiness of the house had been so deafeningly loud that they had slackened into complacency.

The policemen untied Mr Bakshi, the tape unravelling like Draupadi's legendary sari, the more that was pulled off her, the more there was to pull, keeping her honour intact. The two men detailed for the job squatted on either side of the bed and got into a work rhythm—one threw the tape over the bed, the other hurled it from under. Over and under they went, over and under, until the onlookers were mesmerized into believing in the eternity of the moment. The moment snapped when the tape ran out.

Mr Bakshi stood up uncertainly, like an infant who has just discovered the ability to stand. The blood in his legs was put back into circulation with vigorous rubbing.

✠

Family and friends had gathered at his house when they learnt that he had been found. They were all going to participate in the happy homecoming. Mrs Bakshi, Harish, Sarita, Tejpal, Harpreet, Balli, Meiyang, and many others who had attended those parties at his house.

Some were now a little scared of being seen in the company of one who was obviously in bad odour with terrorists, but they went nevertheless. 'Doesn't look nice,' said one. 'I have drunk so much of his scotch that we might as well go and see him, though sometimes I do think that these Hindus have brought it upon themselves.'

The drawing room had been cleared of furniture, carpets, statues, lamps, cut glass. In the middle of that uncharacteristic starkness sat a pandit before a fire, surrounded by pots and pans with varying measures of ghee, lentils, rice and shakkar in them, a banana and an out-of-season Chinese apple with a price sticker firmly glued on to it. He was in attendance to perform the rituals of purification and thanksgiving. He started reciting slokas when the time was just right according to the calendar for auspicious and inauspicious moments, lightly touching each of the ingredients before him as he proceeded to make an imaginary, metaphoric meal to propitiate the gods above. There would be fruit and dessert to follow—for the gods and for everybody else.

The police drove Mr Bakshi in. His entry was much more stately than his exit, but he would never live down the ignominy of having been treated like a sack of potatoes. He sat through the ceremony that had been lined up for him but could not be counted amongst the living after that.

'After all, just breathing, sleeping, eating and shitting does not mean that one is alive,' Mrs Bakshi would whisper to all those who subsequently came to ask after him. And then, in a significantly louder voice, she would tell them all about his exemplary courage: 'He had them pinned to the wall,' she would say. That is what he would have said, had he been able.

His movements had acquired a slow viscousness, as though he was moving in a dream. Gone was that aplomb and bluster which was so much the subject of ridicule behind his back and which was sorely missed now that it was gone. It is so much easier to value things and people who are no longer around, than to cope with the daily drudgery of their presence.

'Bauji ganje ho ke aaye hain,' said their cook, noticing Mr Bakshi's suddenly balding pate, which had become more prominent over his captivity.

But at least he had been found.

15

Balli's marriage had been on hold for some time. One reason for this was that his mother had passed away and there had to be a decent interval between death and festivity. Not that Balli felt that marriage was any reason to celebrate. He also had to admit that he felt quite badly about his mother. Hers had been an unhappy life and an unhappy death. Of course, dying can never be edifying but she seemed to be wrestling with something or someone as she left. And he could only stand by and watch helplessly as she flailed her arms in what seemed like self-defence.

The other reason, not quite convincing as reasons go, but Balli insisted on its validity, was that Mr Bakshi had gone missing.

'What has that got to do with you?' his father had asked him. 'He disappeared so he disappeared. It is not like you have put him in your pocket while everyone is looking for him.'

I cursed him, thought Balli, not particularly keen to voice sentiment born of convoluted, emotionally charged reasoning. His father would not have understood. His logic traversed a fairly straight, unsentimental path.

When it came to his son, however, he did betray occasional

traces of that unsavoury stuff called emotion. For the well-being of Balli he had even commissioned twenty-one Akhand Paths, non-stop readings, cover to cover, of the Guru Granth Sahib at the local gurdwara. The bhai who had made the opening was a particulary pious man. He had covered his mouth with a handkerchief all through the performance of his priestly duties to ensure that he did not shower any spittle onto the holy book, though that did mean that his recitation of the verses was an indistinct murmur, especially for those who had chosen to make the effort of sitting there to listen to him. From there on, it was a line-up of Sikh priests who took the baton one by one and completed the relay reading in forty-two hours. One reading of the Granth Sahib took a well documented forty-eight hours. Perhaps someone had measured it with a trip meter at some point of time. But the priests engaged by Balli's father had obviously made short work of it.

In spite of having outsourced it all, the reading and venue, Balli's father had not even a fleeting moment of doubt that the blessings that might accrue thereof would get deposited into the account of the hanky-holding priest instead of working towards getting Balli married.

'Now Mr Bakshi is back,' he said, looking meaningfully at Balli, as they drove back from the homecoming. 'What a lot of smoke!' he remarked. And then, for good measure, resorted to an English idiom, which did not have very much to do with the course of events except in a purely physical sense. 'There can be no smoke without fire,' he said, looking pleased with the aptness of his expression. The tongues of fire in the havan kundli had nearly slurped at the ceiling. The folds of the turban that layered his forehead were drenched in sweat and he had had to suppress frequent bouts of coughing occasioned by the rising smoke that filled the room. It was an act of uncharacteristic politeness and delicacy on his part because, at most other times, he would have let loose without a qualm, giving everyone present the full benefit of infected air.

'Yes, he is back,' said Balli. 'But he does not seem to be quite his normal self. And Kailla is still missing.'

'Sisterfucker. You are now going to give me that as a reason for not getting married?'

Sensing a moment of weakness he quickly increased the pressure, resorting to a small measure of emotional blackmail to gain acquiescence.

'Your mother, if she were alive today—and who knows, she may even now be keeping an eye on things from up there— would be so happy to know that you are getting married.'

And, in fact, he was quite hoping that she was actually looking on since he was no longer visiting his mistress in Manali. The fizz in that one had evaporated. It was stealth that had aerated his extramarital relationship.

Balli buckled to the possibility of his mother's celestial blessings.

It was settled then. Balli would marry Girl Number Two. He would have to stop calling her that and try to get used to her name: Paramjot. Though maybe, he had unknowingly fathered a trend. Sowed a seed. Two years later, film directors in Bombay discovered the formula but with a difference. *Hero No. 1, Khiladi No. 1, Biwi No. 1, Jodi No. 1.* The films were a great success with audiences. And everything and everyone was numero uno. None of this substandard business of being second. But Balli was never encumbered by such aspirations. He had settled for Girl Number Two. And really, the trend was all that he would ever father.

They got married. It was a hurried affair since Balli's father wanted to rush through with it before the onset of second thoughts.

The alliance was doomed from the start. Fissures ran in all directions, including the realm of procreation, though they continued to live together in average matrimonial disharmony.

Paramjot was very keen to have a child. He was not. Paramjot was driven by the instinct to mother. He was wary of fatherhood. This became a growing argument. It quickly grew out of its infancy and was soon on its feet, becoming an ominous presence between them. Balli had managed to shake off the buzz in his head about birds and bees, overcoming his hesitation about matters sexual. But he found it difficult to explain to his wife why he did not want a child.

On his wedding night he came up with the idea of boiling his balls instead of insisting on contraception. As a schoolboy he had digested his textbooks well. The minimal science he had studied had taught him that sperm, born and bred in the testicles, need cool climes to survive. That is why testicles hang outside the heat of the body to provide them an abode. He filled a mug with hot water from the geyser and held his balls in it, hoping to zap to zilch those tiny emissaries of life, before he went to bed.

'Ahhhhhhhhhh,' he said. It was scalding. The wedding night was a success. All the sperm had been incinerated.

16

'But where is Kailla?' said Jassi, as she looked up from her game of solitaire.

Lately, she had taken to regarding the game as a sort of nemesis. Kailla had bought the pack for her on one of his jaunts in the market. His purchases were legendary. A bit surreal, a bit gratuitous, a bit outlandish, and a bit creative— and utterly useless most of the time. A torch that worked as a cigarette lighter though no one smoked, a pair of scissors with an inbuilt bottle opener though no one drank anything aerated, a key chain that said 'here I am' if you clapped loudly though the house was never locked. Everything he bought had to be able to do or display any two disparate things.

'Cards?' she asked him. 'What will I do with them? I am not a gambler.'

She was only voicing a well-entrenched prejudice. Good people did not play cards.

'Move this card, this way and now that way,' he said excitedly, showing her the three-dimensional image on its back. 'See, this baby becomes a full-grown man, depending upon which way you look at it.'

He was totally taken up with his find.

'Keep them,' he said. 'You might need them sometime.'

They were useful now. She would sit cross-legged on her bed in meditation mode, slide the cards out from under her pillow and pat them into position. The cards, laid out in front of her in neat rows in descending order, in alternating colours, kept her occupied and stopped her from thinking about things that she could not bear to think about. She would keep to the rules. No cheating. Not even with herself. But Kailla's disappearance was an unhappiness within, which needed a certain sleight of emotions. There she had to cheat. When she caught herself wondering about the whereabouts of Kailla and agonizing, she would play the cards in her head, moving imaginary sequences up and down. She could even line up people, varying in sex, age, habits—people offered many more colours than the limited four of a pack of cards—and she could shuffle them around. Her father, her mother, Kailla, Harpreet, all those who were a part of her life and all those others who had been in and out of it, and even those she knew of but had never seen. Each move threw up a brilliant explosion of memories and possibilities, of odd combinations and mismatches or reassurances. She placed her husband and that other woman in one of the sequences. If her husband had married that other woman he would have been at the gurdwara every evening, praying, because that is what she did. Or then, alternately, she might have taken to whisky because that is what he did every evening. Or then, they each might have carried on doing what they each did, and scoffed at the other. He was engaged to the other girl before he married Jassi. The engagement broke off and just as well it did, otherwise their home would have resonated with the clanging of swords. Jassi liked speculating gleefully on the sound of the clash. And though she had a name, Jassi still thought of her only as 'that other woman'.

I have saved my husband from the excesses of devotion—of that paradoxical elevation of spirit occasioned by rubbing ones nose in dust. 'The guilty bows double,' she thought, summoning lines from the Asa-di-var, a collection of hymns in the Guru Granth Sahib which added up to a code of conduct for daily life. It was meant to be read in the morning and that is just what she did, enjoying the ordinariness and yet profundity of thought.

This play of people as cards was an absorbing diversion.

'Kailla?' she asked, as Harpreet and Tejpal walked in after their daily round of police stations. If God above had brought back Bakshi, then he should also have conjured up Kailla, she thought. He, at least, should be able to do two things simultaneously, otherwise his being God did not count for very much. Any two divergent things. And Bakshi and Kailla were very different people. He should be able to bring them out of his hat or turban or whatever it was that he wore. Bakshi was back and she expected Kailla to walk in the door next.

✹

In Tejpal's dreams, the ones in which he had to catch his breath, the old man being tossed up in the air was increasingly beginning to look like Kailla, and he knew that he had to find Kailla or he would be on a nightmare run for the rest of his life.

Harpreet watched Tejpal heaped in front of the television, his neck sinking into his chest, his chest sinking into his stomach, his stomach sinking into his crotch, neither asleep nor awake, neither prone nor upright, with the remote control for the television firmly in his hand. That she felt a heaving of emotion, of caring even for this strange contortionist, meant perhaps that they had a good marriage and had been married long enough to absorb quirks and smelly farts and incipient potbellies. She tried to gently wrest the remote from him. He immediately sprang back to life, into a predatory wakefulness. He was not going to part with it.

'What are you doing?' he said angrily, as though she had transgressed a sacrosanct boundary.

But as soon as he woke up, he was asleep again. His sleeping finger accidentally jabbed at buttons, and channels jumped in and out of the television like fleas on a dog. When surfing stopped momentarily with yet another involuntary jab, they were beaming—the miracle of Lord Ganesha statues drinking milk. They said that a man had woken up early morning that day, dreaming that Lord Ganesha was thirsty and wanted milk. He rushed to the temple to find that the lord was quaffing it down. They said that it was a sign, a very good sign. Hysterical devotees were lining up everywhere.

Ruling party politicians said that it was the far right drumming up yet another god, from Lord Ram to Lord Ganesha, for the Lok Sabha elections.

Opposition party politicians said that a ruling party loyalist had thought the whole thing up to try and divert attention from criminal charges levelled against him.

People in Toronto said that a poor country like India should be feeding the milk to its hungry millions instead of spooning it out to Lord Ganesha.

He was drinking milk at the Mangal Mandir in Montgomery County Maryland, in Southall, in Malyasia, in Thailand, in Nepal, in Bangladesh, in Italy where they were in any case used to Virgin Mary's statue weeping blood.

Officials from the Ministry of Science and Technology cleverly fed the god coloured milk and found that it coated the statue after being sucked up by capillary action. But no one was interested in scientific home truths just then. It was time for an overflow of imagination.

Drains ran milk.

Milk vendors only said 'Balle, balle', performing a joyous bhangra as they sold more and still more milk.

Harpreet looked away from the television but a chiaroscuro continued to dance in her peripheral vision. At the stroke of midnight Lord Ganesha stopped sipping milk, as one of the news anchors had delicately put it, and now the twenty-four-hour news channels were only repeating themselves, letting the same feed run on and on. Perhaps the man at the controls could finally doze, having put the news channel on autopilot.

Tejpal was also dozing. When awake he had wondered why they had not offered the god whisky instead. An ancient god and why, at his age, would he want to drink milk? A few pegs of whisky would have been more appropriate. It might have made for better public relations when they ultimately reported to the heavens above. With that philosophical thought, he had poured himself his daily round of unrestrained whisky and lulled himself into a semi-stupor.

Under the sink in the kitchen, empty bottles stood in a dense grid awaiting the raddi wala. 'Radiiiia, paper walaa, akhbaar, radiiiie,' he would call out in a strange guttural as he cycled past slowly. And still more slowly past their gate. He knew that there was a rapid accumulation of empties in this house and if he hovered around long enough and called out long enough, summoning a voice from the depths of his being, Harpreet would finally emerge. Somebody here sure drank with the appetite of a dehydrated sponge. However, he would not pass judgement. He would only put the whisky, beer and rum bottles in a man-sized gunny sack, their mouths, necks and torsos tossed around carelessly, their protuberances rubbing each other every which way, and carry them away in a cascade of tinkling sounds. He would pay her the appropriate amount for them.

Recycling comes so naturally to us, thought Harpreet, while the West kicks up such a storm about it but only manages to make mountains of discarded cans and cartons. The retreating back of the raddi wala made her philosophical, though she was really thinking about Tejpal and his constant date with the past, the ghosts that danced in his head, the recycling of memories.

Tejpal's head rolled leeward, buffeted by the storm in his mind, his eyelids curtained down, his arm losing its tautness, and he was asleep again.

She hoped that he would get up in time for their appointment with a police official in the ongoing search for Kailla. But she knew that she too would not sleep.

17

'He is a telephone.' That is what people said of the police official whom Harpreet and Tejpal met the next morning. 'There it sits, innocent, passively mute, until someone rings.'

It sounded suspiciously harmless but also ineffectual. That is not how a policeman was expected to be. He was supposed to be ruthless and remorseless and proactive, if not in matters of policing, then at least in matters of amassing wealth. But this one seemed to have been struck dumb, looking at them with large sorrowful eyes. Only later they learnt that he was the strong, silent type—that his silence was only a strategy to intimidate, to pre-empt any ambitious notions of proximity that chattiness might induce and to ensure that his visitors shifted uncomfortably in their chairs. He processed each word deep inside his stomach before he let it see the light of day.

'They say that in his childhood, he used to skin cats alive,' whispered a harried fellow supplicant waiting outside. 'A child prodigy, who knew just what he was going to be doing when he grew up.'

What nobody knew was that in his backyard he had a huge cage of a size which might house a lion. He had enough space for the extravagance of the cage. Government housing was generous to its chosen few. In that cage were hundreds of love birds in myriad colours. Blue and green and yellow, with white crests. Their chirping and flapping filled the atmosphere. He had brought back a pair once and they had multiplied into profusion. Whenever he came back from a bloody encounter with insurgents, the kind that involved cold-blooded killing, he would shut himself in the cage and sit quite still, letting the birds assume that he was only one of the many perches. When he emerged from there he was ready to proceed from where he had left off.

Harpreet and Tejpal had got the appointment through Balli's father's second cousin's daughter, who was married to the official's son.

'You see, it is part of the drill,' he said with an uplifted finger. 'A crime—and—just like that,' he snapped his fingers for a graphic representation of their speed, 'we pick up people—for questioning—those on our files and some others who have been seen loitering about. Nothing personal. You get my point?'

The measured cadences should have had some sinister music playing in the background. Both of them could see the words frosting over.

'Karnail Singh, you said his name was?'

'Yes. We call him Kailla though,' Harpreet said.

He did not think that women should be let loose on the world in this brazen manner. He would have been much more comfortable if Tejpal had come alone.

'You will forgive me,' he said, joining his hands in supplication, 'but you may call him what you like, that is really not my concern. I will check.' The exaggerated politeness only enhanced the sense of affront that he felt on being addressed by a woman.

He made a phone call. Spoke less. Heard more. He said in an ominous undertone with his lips virtually kissing the instrument, 'Karnail Singh. Find out about him.'

And then he went into listening mode. Not an achha, haan or yes or even a soundless hmm escaped his steely lips. The voice on the other side must have known him well enough to presume his continued presence at the end of the line. Tejpal and Harpreet fidgeted. They examined their hands, Harpreet spun her ring around on her finger, Tejpal opened and shut the clasp of his watch, both minutely studied the wall behind the official, hoped for a revelatory sign from the chief minister's portrait hanging on it. They tried to listen intelligently to the meaning of the enveloping silence and wore themselves down to taut yet quivering strings by the time he had finished.

With slow deliberateness, like someone running a forty-eight frames per second recording on twenty-four, his actions played themselves out. His manner invested the whole humdrum business of making a phone call, restoring the handset to its cradle and leaning back in a chair with such heavy import, that when he did finally turn around to them, the moment seemed potent with meaning. As though they were now going to understand eternity, plug into the timeless and feel the heartbeat of the universe.

'He is no longer in our custody. We released him the next day.'

'But where...' began Harpreet.

A finger went up, silencing them. Both of them immediately cowered into compliance.

'Policing these days is difficult business. On some occasions there is no time for niceties. When there are killings and kidnappings we have no time to make polite inquiries over a cup of tea and a pleasant conversation about the weather and then casually ask, "Where do you plan to drop the next bomb, or shoot the next set of innocents?", or then, as in this case, "Where have you hidden the gentleman you picked up from his house?" And mistakes are made which have to be understood as such. Don't quote me on this though. I am telling you all this only because you are…' his voice faded, trying to explain the connection, and ended lamely with, '… you come recommended by known quarters.'

It was uncharacteristic verbosity on his part, but then, as he had said, they had come with a sifarish and that is what had made him open his heart out, the contents of which would be regarded as limited fare in others, but in his case was a clearance sale.

When Tejpal and Harpreet left, they knew even less than when they had come. Kailla was no longer in jail and that closed an inquiry point.

'But where then is Kailla?' said Harpreet, completing her query of a while ago.

18

Kailla never really came back and if he did, he continued to elude everyone. There were many who claimed to have seen him but he had become a rumoured presence, like a whisper in the wind.

'You know my chachaji told me that Kailla was seen near the clock tower...'

Tejpal and Harpreet would jump to it. They would meet the said chachaji who would direct them to a friend he had met at a party, who would then show them to a neighbour's house, where the sighting would be ascribed to a visiting niece who would then be rung up, only to say that she had somehow got this impression when they were all talking about it and someone seemed to have mentioned something to that effect...

Kailla was seen watching a movie, *Beqabu Pyar,* in his favourite Society cinema in Chaura Bazaar. This Bhojpuri film about unrestrained love had so caught his attention that his jaw had dropped a few significant inches. The cleaning woman who came to Harpreet's house told her that her daughter-in-law had seen him.

'Was driving down and saw him, or someone who looked like him, disappearing round the corner, into that little lane that goes to the Masjid-do-manzili. But the traffic was so snarled just then, that I could not stop,' said Balli's father.

'Beeji, he was having himself photographed in that Rajhans Studio in Dhakka Colony,' said the woman who came to give Jassi her weekly oil massage. One of those no-good young men who loiter around street corners as a whole time occupation and do nothing else, had told her.

'Kailla? No, no. Not possible. Must have been someone else. Kailla never even looked at himself in the mirror, why would he want to have himself photographed?' said Jassi. She knew there was some mistake here.

However, she did recall that one spring-cleaning day, she had come upon Kailla critically examining himself in a photo frame. He had taken down a painting from the wall, about to dust it. The painting was of the legendary lovers Sohni and Mahiwal by Sobha Singh, which was a must-have in old houses that had not yet been done over by interior decorators. It had become powder at the base of the frame just as soon as he had unhooked it from its nail. Termites had been working on it and the print was only holding together in a temporary truce. The minute it was moved it had crumbled to dust. And Kailla had found himself looking at his own reflection.

Sweety did not see him again, though she wished she had. What if she had taken up the offer he had come with? And as she pirouetted on the stage, catching her audience in a whirl, she wondered if she could ever stand around holding a glass, looking half bored, half expectant, through a whole evening and half the night. She was too much of a bred-on-the-ground realist to be nurturing any fancies about a fairy-tale transformation in her life. But, no harm done in dreaming. What if Kailla had come to wave a magic wand?

But of course, she had no idea that he had disappeared and that it needed a whoosh of that same wand to bring him back in the first place.

Meiyang wondered if living between identities could make one invisible. He checked in the mirror every morning, pinched himself, as did his mirror image, to make sure that he was still around. He had obviously not become vapour as had Kailla.

It was November once more and the air was beginning to smell of roasted peanuts. The ground was strewn with peanut peels which crackled underfoot on sidewalks, and movie theatres and the atmosphere crackled with the sound of exploding fireworks in anticipation of Diwali.

It was time to take out woollens for yet another approaching winter. The bedding would have to be overturned to open the box bed, naphthalene balls dislodged from the folds of pullovers, the smell of dry-cleaning filling the air as coats were unbuttoned and hung up. And once again Harpreet remembered that she must call in the carpenter to fashion a stay for the lid of the box bed. It was a recurring thought, an annual thought, a November thought, which evaporated every summer. But come November she would ask Tejpal to hold the lid up while she doubled into the cavity to pull out the woollens. And he would complain yet again, about this ridiculous routine in which he was essentially called upon to simulate a car hood support. He would grumble the whole time and she would think about the carpenter while he grumbled. She would call the carpenter tomorrow morning, she would resolve. But by morning there were always many other things to claim her attention and she would forget. The box beds had been made in the November of 1985 to economize on space, because they were already beginning to accumulate the unnecessary baggage of a long stay and were finding it difficult to compact themselves into those two rooms.

Tejpal and Harpreet did not see Kailla even once. Maybe gullibility would help, thought Harpreet. Had Kailla turned into a pestle? But Justice Kailla had decreed that to be a punishment, and why would anyone want to punish Kailla? A butterfly then, one of the many who fluttered around in this season, one of the yellow ones like shooting stars in their green firmament, impossible to pin down with a watching eye? The thought was ridiculous. Even gullibility could not be stretched this far and poetry could not be a substitute for life.

Jassi put the last ace in place and waited.